Relief

Relief

Anna Taylor

Victoria University Press

VICTORIA UNIVERSITY PRESS
Victoria University of Wellington
PO Box 600 Wellington
http://www.victoria.ac.nz/vup

National Library of New Zealand Cataloguing-in-Publication Data

Taylor, Anna, 1982-
Relief / Anna Taylor.
ISBN 978-0-86473-587-4
I. Title.
NZ823.3—dc 22

Published with the assistance of a grant from

Printed by Printlink, Wellington

For my mother, Erin,
with all my love and gratitude

Contents

Working Girl

In the summer of 1985 Ellie spent most days two houses along, at Mr Fin's. It was hot that summer, hotter than usual, and everyone in the street kept their sprinklers going, day after day, the long wisps of water moving lazily back and forth across the lawns.

Ellie got a new bike for Christmas, a two-wheeler, and she rode it down to Jefferson's corner and back every morning before breakfast. Once, she and her sister went beyond that point, right up the hill past Mr and Mrs Mildenhall's, and on the way back a man in a clattery car turned around and drove, slowly, right beside them, his bare arm dangling out the open window, a fag puffing in the corner of his mouth.

'I'll race you,' Laura hissed. 'I'll race you all the way home,' and even though Ellie was on her old bike then, with trainer wheels on, she knew it wasn't a game, and pedaled with all her might, the muscles in her legs getting hot, and stretching and stretching, like rubber bands.

Mr Fin had moved in at the end of 1982, when Ellie was four. His was the second to last section to go in the street. It lay just beyond Mr Ford's gravelly, snaky driveway, beside the bamboo grove. Ellie could see the bamboo from her bedroom window, and before Mr Fin arrived she went across there sometimes in her gumboots to muck around in the puddles. It was all clay over there, with tufts of scrappy grass by the fenceline, and after a solid night of rain the ground would get slippery—its top layer a silky tan—and she was able to slip and slide all over the place, the mud curling up over the ridged soles of her boots and splattering across her legs.

Mr Fin knocked on their door two weeks after the SOLD sticker had been pasted over the sign at no. 38. Laura was off school with the mumps that day, and Ellie wasn't allowed to go to kindy. They were hanging around in the living room, squares of morning sun lying flat on the floor; their Mum was still in her dressing gown, her hair dark and wet from the shower. The knock gave them a fright. Who could it be?

Ellie went to check.

Mr Fin stood in the doorway, one shoulder leaning

casually against the frame. He filled it all up, blocking the view of the concrete path with its patch of lawn on either side, and the gate leading to the pavement and the road. She blinked up at him.

'Morning miss!' he said, and extended his hand.

She didn't reach out hers. She fiddled with the doorknob.

'Is your Mum home?'

Ellie didn't know what to say. She shifted on her feet and breathed very quietly. She thought, Laura would say yes, yes-she-is, wait-a-moment-please. But she couldn't quite find the words; her tongue felt thick and fat.

'Perhaps,' he smiled at her, quietly, 'it's you who's the lady of the house, eh?'

Ellie nodded. That seemed the best thing to do. But it only made Mr Fin laugh.

'Thought so,' he said. 'Thought so.'

And then there was just silence. He cleared his throat.

'Well I'm just over the way there,' he said, pointing, 'and I guess you could say I was kind of in the neighbourhood.' And then he laughed again.

'I should probably just go, your highness,' he said. 'That's probably best.'

At that moment there was a scuffling sound down the hallway and Ellie's Mum appeared, dressed, to save the day. She had tied her wet hair back and flashed some lipstick across her mouth.

He put out his hand to her, and she shook it.

'Me and the missus have been having a good little chat,' he said. 'I'm Finley. Thought I should just come on over to introduce myself.'

Ellie's Mum smiled brightly. 'Of course!' she said. 'God, excuse the mess!'

She invited him in for tea.

Mr Fin wore a satchel of tools slung over his shoulder, and smelt of wood and something stronger too—yeasty bread. His singlet hung low and loose, flapping carelessly under his arms. He strode inside and leaned against the bench. Ellie and Laura could hear the rumble of his voice moving through the walls from the kitchen. Their Mum's, slightly shrill and tense, was as clear as a bell.

'It's a lovely neighbourhood,' she said. 'You'll fit in just fine.'

They went out on the deck.

Ellie and Laura hung around inside, listening to the clinking of porcelain against porcelain. Splinters of dust, lit up by the sun, did a slow whirly swirl in the air. Laura got out the board games. They settled themselves down.

On the way back inside, Mr Fin's knees and his tanned thick thighs nearly walked right into their jigsaw.

'Excuse me-e,' he exclaimed. 'Two such dainty little ladies almost blending right on into the carpet.'

Ellie's mother laughed. 'In the middle of the room,' she said. '*Right* in the way.'

'But how could I ever have missed them,' he said. 'Little ladies such as these. And doing a jigsaw of the—' he squinted— 'of the . . .'

'Leaning Tower of Pisa,' Laura said helpfully.

'Leaning Tower of Pisa, no less.' He crouched down close beside them, so that Ellie had to tuck her chin into her chest and turn her eyes away.

He swayed there, on his haunches, from side to side.

'Looks like I look,' he said, 'when I've been running round all night, painting the town. Not that I'd do that now, ma'am.' He clicked his tongue at Laura and her lumpy neck. 'No siree.'

'Have you ever seen it?' Ellie's mother said. 'The tower, I mean.'

Mr Fin tapped his fingers on the ground. He didn't answer her.

'Actually,' he said, 'would you have a look at this?' He paused, and raised and dropped his eyebrows several times. 'What have I got in here?'

Ellie didn't look, not directly anyway, but out of the corner of her eyes she saw Mr Fin's hand reach into his pocket and come out clasping one, and then two, tightly wrapped sweets. They shimmered on his palm like little jewels.

'Say thank you,' their mother said, and Laura said, thank-you-very-much, but Ellie sat stock still, her feet tucked neatly under herself, and she still didn't say thank you when he placed the lolly on the floor beside her knee, close enough for her fingers to reach out, slowly, towards the crackly red of its wrapping.

*

1985 was the year Ellie was in Mr Slater's class, and also the year her best friend moved to Australia, every now and then sending home letters covered with thick coloured stamps. Ellie didn't know any of that yet—what was to come, stuck in that endless summer of sun with nothing to do. A girl called Katie-Ann Small went missing that summer, in a town Ellie had never heard of. She caught a snippet of the news one night, before her parents hurriedly switched it off, showing her—this Katie-Ann—wearing a pink summer dress with a white trim, and smiling so hard it looked like her teeth had nothing to hold them in and could come clattering out of her mouth any minute like a broken string of pearls.

Someone who didn't have the right had taken her— that's what abduction meant, Ellie's mother said. Laura started carrying nail scissors in her pocket wherever she went. Just in case someone tried to abduct her too.

Every Sunday, everybody but Mr Fin would mow their lawns. The hum and whir of the mowers would join in with the creaking cicadas and, Ellie's mother said, it was just about enough to make you go deaf or mad, all that noise. Ellie's Dad brought the fan from his office home in the weekends, and they set it up in the lounge and took turns standing in front of it, the drum of its arms, going round and round, mixing with the sound in their chests. She liked the way its head moved from side to side as if it were saying no, and she stood closer and closer to it, until her Mum said, 'Watch out. What if your hair got caught?' And raised her eyebrows. 'Imagine that, Ellie.'

The fan was a silvery grey, with three red buttons, and from that moment on it turned into something beginning with D—for Danger. Ellie didn't stand close to it any more. She walked through the room as far away from it as she could get. Every Friday, when her Dad appeared in the doorway, the cool metallic of the fan in his arms, she was filled up with its presence, right down to her toes. As he plugged it in, and turned the switch, she could feel herself being drawn towards it, her hair getting caught up, flapping like ribbons, and her body lifting up off the ground, moving towards the clack and the whir, right into the middle of that cold beating wind.

Mr Fin didn't mow his lawns on Sunday because he didn't have any. He didn't *believe* in lawns, he told Ellie once. But, really, she thought, it was because he was building his house out the front of his section and living in a one-room shack out the back, and with all the to-ing and fro-ing the lawns just didn't have a chance—the blades of grass were trampled back in under the clay every time they tried to squeeze their heads through its dry, cracked surface. Mr Fin's house was taking ages to get built. It was because he was doing it all himself, even the plumbing. It was just a shell, really, looking whole and complete from the outside but all hollowed out when you stepped in the front door. The floor was concrete, covered in shavings of wood, and there were no walls, just beams surrounding the toilets and the bath, a staircase with no rail, a pile of bricks where the fireplace would be. If you squinted your eyes real tight, Mr Fin said, you could almost imagine it, *see* it, finished. But Ellie couldn't. She tried once and everything looked just the same, but blurry.

Next door to Mr Fin were Wayne Hiles and his Indian wife, Jhumpa. They lived in the biggest house in the street, a stucco mansion with a tall wooden door. Jhumpa, Ellie thought, was the prettiest lady she knew. Her hair was thick and black and seemed to stay up, coiled into a fat bun, all by itself. She did not wear a sari like the Indian women Ellie had seen at the gift shop in Main Street, but wore brightly coloured tops threaded with gold, and matching skirts, and shoes that made a pitter-patter sound when she walked. She had gold bangles on one arm, almost reaching right up to her elbow, and rings on every finger. Ellie's Mum said she didn't know what Jhumpa was doing with Wayne Hiles—who was not pretty at all—but she thought it could possibly have something to do with the M word. Money.

They had a goldfish almost as big as Ellie's head that they fed cake to straight off their plates.

That summer, Jhumpa began to sing by the open window of her bathroom, for the benefit, everyone thought, of Mr Fin. Laura said it was just because she was happy, because where she came from it was always very hot, and this heat, thick and heavy, reminded her of being at home, and made her want to open her mouth to let the joy out.
It was strange, though, how she always started at 9.30, just as Mr Fin was stepping outside in his baggy singlet and grubby shorts and rough working boots. And also how she sang for a good hour or so, long after the steam from her shower had stopped puffing in rolling white clouds out the open window.

Ellie wondered about India, and why the thought of it—with its thick, sweet drink that Jhumpa had once given her to try, and its oily crackers, round as pancakes—would make anyone want to sing that much.

*

In early January, in the afternoons, the tar on the edge of the road began to melt. It was about then that Ellie started going over to Mr Fin's on a regular basis. Holidays had sort of lost their sheen. Laura was too busy hanging round with her friends to notice her; she suddenly didn't even want to go for bike rides in the morning, even though Ellie had her new bike with a bell on it. Ellie's Mum got more and more tired—it was the heat, she said—and she began to lie down a lot on the couch in the living room.

Mr Fin called out to Ellie on her third lap of the street one morning.

'Ellie H,' he said. 'Getting yourself some air?'

He was surveying his house from the edge of the pavement, a cup of coffee between his hands.

She was nervous of the brakes, they were so strong she had just about gone over the handlebars, twice, so she didn't stop, just nodded vigorously and kept going.

The next day, though, he was out the front again, planting shrubs along the fence-line.

'You're going to cut a track in the footpath, Ellie H,' he said, 'going up and down like that all day. Want a job?'

Ellie, who didn't think six-and-a-half-year-olds were things that anybody would ever want to have around, stuck her brakes on and lurched to a halt.

'Yes, please. Thank you,' she said. Just like her mother had taught her.

That morning Mr Fin got her to help him with the plants. He dug a hole while she stood beside him, holding a mini tree in her arms, its waxy leaves against her chest. When the hole was ready he pulled on the black plastic wrapper that held the tree's dirt in. They patted the earth down together.

'Tell me something, Ellie H,' he said.

And Ellie, who thought maybe talking was part of her job, told him about Tom Birch, who had something wrong in his chest and had fallen over on the field one day, flat on his face. He'd got out of Jump Rope for Heart, which everyone else had to do, and was allowed to read books instead. She wished that she had something wrong there too.

Mr Fin laughed.

'What's your favourite country?' he said.

She said she didn't really know.

'If you had wings—' he leaned past her for the watering can— 'where would you fly to, little Miss E? Anywhere in the world.'

Ellie didn't know much about the world, or about wings. She'd never even seen an aeroplane apart from on TV. She paused. She thought about Jhumpa.

'Prob-ly India,' she said.

'India, eh? Like elephants?'

She nodded.

'Well I'll tell you what, Ellie H,' he said. 'Next time I go off to India, I'll pop you in my pocket. I'll take you too.'

Mr Fin almost had a wife. Almost—because they weren't married yet, but were going to be, one day. Her name was Mindy Malone and she lived in Jacksonville, America, that's where she was from. Mr Fin said he was building the house for her, for Mindy. Just like the guy and the Taj Mahal. He took Ellie inside and rifled under his bed, and found an atlas that had a picture of the Taj Mahal in its front. It was pearly white and looked like a castle. She touched it with her fingers. Mr Fin held the page open with his big, hairy hand.

'Inside,' he said, 'it's always cool, even in the heat.' He gestured towards the open door. 'Hotter than this, little Miss E.'

He read out the caption from underneath. 'The Taj Mahal is the greatest monument to love,' it said. 'Some call it the most romantic building in the world.'

Mr Fin made a sound of agreement in his throat and flicked forward to the maps.

The United States of America was big and fat, with lots of different coloured squares and only a thin trim of blue around the corners. He pointed to a tiny dot on its edge.

'Mindy's right there,' he said. 'Right now. Little darlin'.'

Ellie watched how he moved his head close to the map, as if he could see her, as if he had her pinned firmly under his finger, like a bug. She tried to imagine what his Little Darling would look like, and how small the place she was living in must be, such a tiny dot in such a swamp of land.

At the back of Mr Fin's section was a line of tall bamboo trees that curled around the edge of his one-roomed house. They were so thin they swayed in even the lightest breeze, making the long leaves rustle like paper. Ellie had heard somewhere that panda bears ate nothing but bamboo for breakfast lunch and dinner, and that in some places there were whole forests of the stuff and nothing else.

Mr Fin said that he was going to make a Japanese-style pond, and that once, in a Japanese garden, he had seen a lantern with a flame in it that never went out. He would take Ellie to the pet store one day, he said, to help him choose the fish, once everything was ready. She could name them too, if she wanted.

*

Wayne and Jhumpa invited the whole street round for a barbecue. To make the most of the weather, they said.

Ellie's Mum said she didn't want to go.

'What an effort,' she said. 'Socialising!'

Ellie and Laura wore the outfits they had worn on Christmas Day. Laura's a cream pant suit with dark green polka dots all over, Ellie's a sky-blue dress with a sailing boat embroidered on the front. She felt like a baby.

Mr Fin was there wearing shorts and a long-sleeved shirt, tucked in, despite the heat. He had a beer in his hand.

'Here she comes,' he said, 'my little working girl.'

Ellie's Mum coughed.

'Wrong choice of words, maybe. Sorry ma'am.' He lifted his hand to his head, as if to tip his hat, but there wasn't one. Ellie's Mum patted his side. They both laughed.

Ellie wanted to say that she *was* a working girl now, Mr Fin had already paid her three dollars, but Jhumpa came along and tweaked her cheek and planted a frosty glass of Fanta in her hand.

Mr and Mrs Mildenhall were there, Mr Mildenhall in his wheelchair since the accident, everyone trying not to stare. The Whitebridges from no. 28 sat in the corner with their two fat babies, twins, one on each lap. Mr Ford stood by the snacks table and looked glumly out the sliding doors at the fountain—a concrete bird with water pulsing out of its upturned beak.

'Wayne drew up the designs for that,' Jhumpa said to him, pronouncing 'that' as if it ended with a 'd'.

Mr Ford said, 'Really?' and ate a sausage roll.

Ellie and Laura stood by the billowing netting curtains, gulping their drinks. The smell of the popping, spitting sausages, cooking out on the deck, wafted in on little gusts. Wayne was busy telling Mr Whitebridge about how Jhumpa had started singing lessons; how he thought she might have the makings of something big. He slid his palm across his thinning hair as he talked.

'Voice of an angel,' he said. 'Great breath control.'

'Keeping us all well entertained,' Ellie's Dad said, 'isn't that right, Finley?' And Ellie's Mum, bouncing one of the babies on her hip, took two side-steps in his direction and kicked the back of his heel.

Neither Wayne nor Jhumpa had heard, thank god, she said later. But what if they had? Mr Fin, leaning against the Steinway piano, said, 'What, indeed,' and raised his glass, making the ice tinkle softly against its sides.

He had a photo of Mindy Malone in his shirt pocket. A recent one. She had sent it over in a package, all the way from Jacksonville, along with the shirt he was wearing, and a cap, he said, with the American flag on it, to keep the sun off.

'It must be so hard for you,' Ellie's Mum said, 'being so far away.'

'I miss her something awful,' said Mr Fin, and he passed the photo round.

She wasn't as pretty as Ellie thought she might be. Her

face was round, slightly soft, and she had a gap between her two front teeth. Her yellow hair was piled on top of her head, tied up with a scrunchy. She held a handwritten sign in front of her chest that said *Miss You Honey!!* and had circles for the dots of the exclamation marks, with little smiling faces.

Mr Fin slid the photo back into his pocket, and sat down on a chair next to where Ellie and Laura were standing. He cupped one hand inside another.

'Your sister,' he said to Laura, 'is quite a wee worker. Busy as a bee.'

Laura chewed on her lip, and raised and dropped her shoulders carelessly.

'She's something else all right,' said Mr Fin.

Ellie looked around at the neighbours, standing in little groups, tipping wine glasses and beer bottles up towards their mouths. She wished he would say it again, louder; maybe stand up on his chair and announce it to the room. Everyone would turn around, she thought, and see her, and see that she was something else all right. They would see her, suddenly illuminated in the corner, glowing a soft gold. And Mr Fin beside her, placing a large heavy crown tenderly on the top of her head.

A week later they went to the pet store. Mr Fin had started on the fishpond, even though there was still so much to do on the house. Mindy wouldn't be able to come for another six months or so, he said. There was plenty of time for everything.

He drove Ellie to town in his ute. She put her best

summer dress on for the occasion, the one with rosebuds on it and bright green leaves. The freshly washed fabric sat stiff against her skin.

'Look at *you*,' Mr Fin said, opening the door for her so she could climb on board. 'What a picture, eh?' He looked happy, she thought, shutting the door firmly once she was in.

'Be back in time for lunch,' her Mum called out. And he nodded and waved. Maybe they could have a treat at the dairy, he said. Just a little one.

Ellie was all buckled up in the front seat, the wind streaming in the open window making her hair flap against her face. The hot vinyl of the seats burnt against the backs of her knees. Her legs jolted from side to side. Mr Fin shot her a wink.

'You can name all but one,' he said. 'One of them's mine. That'll have to be Mindy Malone.'

They drove down past Clifton Road, across the bridge. Ellie couldn't see the river at all but Mr Fin said, 'She's looking dry all right,' and she nodded in agreement.

The seatbelt strap dug in slightly, up her neck and across the edge of her face.

In the pet store there were puppies and kittens and rabbits and guinea pigs, all penned up in little cages. Ellie wanted to take them out to give them a pat, but Mr Fin said you could only do that if you bought one.

They weaved through the shop, to the back, where the fish tanks were in a dark corner. They had lights shining up through the water, making the weed glow as it swayed around in there. There were big fish and little ones, but none of them looked like Jhumpa and Wayne's cake-fed gold one who had started to grow a black lump on the top of its head.

'You can choose five, Miss E,' Mr Fin said.

She watched them for a long time, and some of them, she thought, were watching her too. They swam round and round, flicking their tails so fast she could hardly see them move, opening and shutting their little mouths. Sitting on the pebbles there was a boat that blew bubbles out its top.

Ellie chose a black one with an orange stripe, and a big one with gold scales, and three smaller ones that matched.

They drove home with the fish sitting in a bag on her lap.

'Hold tight!' Mr Fin said.

And Ellie looked down at the water tipping dangerously from side to side, and at the fish flapping their fins, and said, quite loudly, 'I think they want to get out.'

The fishpond, with its Japanese-inspired waterfall and border of boulders, was never completed. Mr Fin drew plans for it and everything, but it just ended up being a round hole in the ground, filled with water. That day, though, he believed in that pond with all his heart.

'Mindy will love it,' he said, standing back proudly, his arms folded in front of his chest. Ellie sat on the ground beside him, the bag of fish at her feet. Mr Fin had bought her an ice-block and its stickiness coated her fingers.

'She loves Japan,' he said. 'The simplicity. And with the bamboo—' he pointed behind his head— 'and that pond. Think we have a bit of a theme here. What do you reckon?'

'Will it have water-lilies?' Ellie asked. The pond in the Town Square did, its surface covered with leaves green as frogs and sharp-petalled flowers.

Mr Fin raised his arms above his head and raised his voice a little too.

'Water-lilies?' he called out. 'Ladies and gentlemen, she wants water-lilies!'

He swooped down then, into a grand bow.

'Then water-lilies,' he said, his head close to the ground, 'she will have.'

*

By the end of January the temperature was reaching the mid-30s, most days. Ellie had earned ten dollars working for Mr Fin. School was due to start on the third of February. There had been no rain for four weeks, and even the sprinklers couldn't stop the grass from getting parched round the edges. All the adults starting moving slower and slower, it seemed, flapping newspapers, straw hats, plastic plates in front of their faces. At night, tucked tightly in bed under nothing but a sheet, Ellie could see the last of the light seeping in below her curtains. Her Dad would go outside with the hose about that time, to try to keep the flowers alive. Sometimes Ellie would sit up and hold the curtain back and watch him stepping back and forth across the edge of the lawn; the grey evening light; the hose spluttering and choking in his hands.

Katie-Ann Small's body was found on 24 January, all

folded up in a bag under the sand. When it was announced on the radio news, Ellie's Mum jolted across the kitchen, patty mixture spread up over her wrists, and placed her two sticky palms, flat, across Ellie's ears. She still heard, though, the news-reader's deep calm voice moving through the slits in her Mum's fingers, and when she went to bed that night she crossed hers tightly and prayed, though she didn't know to whom, that Katie-Ann Small could breathe properly now: that she didn't feel sad and scared, wherever she was.

Ellie kept her money in an envelope inside her favourite book, *Bedtime for Frances*. Sometimes, when no one was looking, she took it out and held it in her hand, feeling the coolness of the coins growing warm against her skin. Laura said, quietly, that if she found where Ellie was hiding the money she'd steal the lot and buy herself ten one-dollar mixtures at the dairy. This made Ellie cry. She wasn't sure what she was going to spend the money on, though. She thought maybe a Real Live Feed-Me Baby, like the one Sarah Strand had, that went to the toilet in its nappies.

On the Friday before school started, Ellie's Mum gave her and Laura a hose-down in the front garden. She couldn't be bothered taking them to the pool, she said, and so they put on their togs and ran up and down squealing, getting prickles in their feet. Up close, the water from the hose was so hard it stung, but when the hose was waved up and down the water seemed to separate, forming into hundreds of little droplets, moving up towards the sky, whoosh-whooshing and then hitting the ground with a soft thud.

Mrs Whitebridge walked by with the babies in a double pushchair. There were circles of sweat on the fabric underneath her arms and between her breasts. She waved her fingers at them.

'Thought I'd go for a walk,' she called out, 'but down to the end of the street's quite enough for me!'

'Need a lie-down?' Ellie's Mum said.

'I wish!'

They both laughed wearily, and Laura flapped her arms and said, 'I've got a prickle, I've got a prickle,' and hobbled onto the front porch.

Ellie said she was going to go over to Mr Fin's, but Laura was whinging and whining and her Mum was scolding, and neither of them seemed to hear.

She wandered out the front gate.

Her wet feet left dark prints on the pavement. She could see the pads, and her toes, but the wetness was swallowed up rapidly by the heat, as if she had never been there. She walked past Mr Ford's long sloping driveway, and hopped the rest of the way to Mr Fin's. The trees they had planted together were looking dry; one of them was dead. She pushed past the flax and onto the worn path leading to his sleep-out.

The sliding door was shut, but the windows were open. He was lying on the couch inside.

'Come on in, Ellie H,' he called out.

She stepped in, sliding the door shut again behind her.

The air was thick, and the sound of flies buzzing around, bumping against the walls and windows, filled the room.

Ellie stood in her damp saggy togs, her towel hanging round her neck. Mr Fin didn't move. He was wearing his underpants. The tops of his thighs were covered in thick blond hair.

'Hot enough for you, little Miss E?' he said. 'Been swimming?'

'Just under the hose.'

'Bet you're nice and cool.' He waggled his feet on the edge of the couch. 'It's pretty darn hot, that's for sure.'

Ellie could feel a drip gathering at the edge of her togs and beginning to slide down the outside of her leg.

'Yep,' she said.

'What can I do for you, Ellie H, my little Trojan? Would you like a drink?' He snapped himself up off the couch, moved towards a box by his fridge. 'An apricot?'

'Yes, please. Thank you.'

She moved towards the box too, and realised that that was where all the flies were coming from. Slightly mushy, bruised apricots were piled high, and a moving shell of black swarmed across them. Mr Fin flapped his arms and they all lifted in unison, and then fell back down, like a deep breath.

He placed a warm apricot in her hand and turned towards the fridge, and Ellie saw that his underpants had tiny holes in the back, and hung down a little.

'Well, I'm going to have a beer,' he announced. 'If no one objects.'

She stood still, holding her apricot, not wanting to look at it or bite, feeling the slight wetness of its broken patch of skin against her palm.

Mr Fin collapsed back onto the couch.

'Gee I'm tired today, Ellie,' he said. 'I really am.'

She nodded.

'So hot, isn't it? And me just building, building, building all day. Christ I'm tired.'

Ellie looked down at the ground and saw that she was dripping all over the place. She tried to move her feet to cover up the patches of wet.

'Look at you in your little togs there,' he said, moving his feet aside and up onto the back of the couch. 'Take a seat, Miss E, take a load off.'

She did, perching right on the edge, her knees tight together, the bruised apricot still sitting in her hand.

'Want a drink?' he said. 'Did I already ask? Jesus.'

Ellie said no thank you, she was fine, but he didn't seem to hear, getting up regardless, knocking his knee slightly against her side.

She sat quite upright, a buzzing in her chest and the buzzing in the room. There was a framed photo of Mr Fin and Mindy Malone on the wall in front of her. They wore matching green caps and had their arms slung casually over each other's shoulders. Mr Fin was smiling hard—Ellie didn't think she'd ever seen him smile that much before—but Mindy wasn't really smiling at all. Her doughy face was quite smooth, and her eyes and mouth were round and open, as if she had just seen something she didn't expect. A panda bear, maybe, in the distance.

Mr Fin came back with a glass of water for her, and tried to lie down again, lifting his legs up and over her head.

'There you go, my girl,' he said. 'Sorted.'

The edge of his leg, scratchy with hair, kept brushing

against her shoulder. Her mouth felt dry. She took a small sip of water.

Out of the corner of her eyes she could see his chest, rising and falling, and his tummy button, and a line of hair snaking down underneath it, right in under the elastic band of his underpants. She took another sip, more of a gulp this time, and rested the coolness of the glass bottom on her knee.

'You're very quiet there, Miss E,' Mr Fin said. 'You all right?'

Ellie nodded. If Laura were here, she thought, she would know what to do. She would poke Ellie in the ribs with her elbow, and point to the apricot and say, eat it, under her breath, and Ellie would. She would have Laura sitting next to her, eating one too. Then they could go home. If Laura was here, they could go home.

She squeezed the apricot in her hand, and felt its skin burst a little more, a pouch of wet flesh moving out into her palm. Its juice drizzled down onto her leg Mr. Fin shifted his foot, the cracked skin of his heel resting, lightly, against the side of her leg. Her mouth tasted salty, almost like blood, and the saliva seemed thick and heavy. She swallowed hard.

Above the sound of the flies, quiet at first, and then rising and rising, Ellie heard a noise, like a cat or a bird: something from outside. Mr Fin lifted his head off the arm of the couch and made a sound in his throat. He'd heard it too. It was Jhumpa.

It was not the morning, and Mr Fin was not working outside, and Jhumpa was not having her shower, but she was singing nonetheless, her voice high and wavering, winding in through the open windows. She was singing for India, maybe; or maybe for Mr Fin; or maybe, even, for Ellie sitting on a damp patch on the couch, her knees and feet pressed tight together.

Mr Fin closed his eyes. With one hand he started pulling bobbles of lint off the edge of the couch, his face quite slack, listening. He looked sort of sad, she thought, breathing so slowly, his curled fingers resting against his chest. She hated her Mum's or Dad's eyes being closed when hers were open. She would lift the lashes out and up, exposing the jelly white of their eyeballs, waking them. But she was glad about Mr Fin, that his were closed, one hand still moving rhythmically, pulling and then flicking the little bobbles onto the floor.

Ellie looked out through the closed door. The half-built fish pond, filled with her fish, was like a bowl in the ground, or a small bath. The wood of Mr Fin's half-built house glowed slightly in the afternoon light, its mirrored windows reflecting back everything outside, a white cloud above it, heaving its way across the sky. She lifted the apricot to her mouth.

Eat it, she said to herself.

Electricity

That spring things grew vigorously, but in an odd way, decay blooming like flower buds. Boulders in riverbeds sprouted algae—thick and slimy—that couldn't be scraped off, even with a stick. Schools of fish were washed up on beaches, their fins adorned with clusters shaped like tiny stars. Scientists were excited—they'd never seen anything like it before, it was a *phenomenon*, they said—but everyone else was disturbed. Seafood sales plummeted all over the country; the local fish and chip shop put up a sign in the window, stating that it would be closed until further notice.

People started cleaning their houses and patios feverishly. When searching for a lost earring one morning, Beth discovered a patch of bright pink mould growing in a perfect circle under her chest of drawers.

The air also seemed odd that spring, as if it were charged, electric. It felt to Beth as if all of them—people, plants, houses, sky—were being held hostage inside an enormous generator. She began to get electric shocks off *anything*. Not just when she closed the car door, but when she pushed *start* on the washing machine, or stacked the plates in the cupboard or, worst of all, once, when she went to give her mother a hug. They jumped away from each other when it happened; jumped away simultaneously like two opposing magnets.

Beth started spending five minutes each morning out on the grass, in bare feet, trying to earth herself. It was James's suggestion, though he said his friend Annabelle had suggested it to him, and she'd never tried it, just read it in a book called *How to Heal Your Self and Your Soul*.

Beth did it religiously, not really knowing if it would help. She went out there in her pyjamas every day at 7.30, before her shower and breakfast. The ground always felt damp at that time but not cold. It was lovely, in a strange way, just standing out there on the green, the static electricity supposedly seeping out through her skin. Lasting the full five minutes was always a challenge, though. Once, she dug her toes into the ground, grinding them in and flicking the dirt out with the stubs of her toes, but when she looked down she saw she'd injured a worm by mistake. One end of its tail—or was it its head, god forbid?—was quite mashed, a fleshy pink poultice in the dirt. It writhed around for a moment and then slithered away, seemingly being sucked back into the earth.

Everyone was troubled by what was happening, but went on with their lives, regardless. 'There's something rotten in the state of Denmark,' James kept saying, jokingly, but even he knew it was no laughing matter. People stopped watching the news, as if reality was some dumb sitcom they wanted nothing to do with any more. *It's not my fault*, they all seemed to be saying under their breath. *It's nothing to do with me. Is it?*

*

On the first Sunday of that October, Beth's brother got married. He brought his fiancée back from Illinois, where they'd been living, and they went to a registry office and got married, just two days after they arrived home. There was absolutely no fuss. They sent out no invitations and didn't have a party afterwards, probably because he'd got her knocked up, their father said, though as time went on it became clear that that wasn't the case. It was typical Will, though, Beth thought. He had just slipped his fiancée into the country as if she were an illegal substance in his bag.

And then there was scandal number two. Four days after the wedding, Will put in an offer on the Landfall Motel—which had been on the market for ten solid months—and got it. He referred to this as his landslide victory, which seemed ironic, though he didn't mean it that way. The Landfall Motel was living up to its name. It was down by the river, and the banks were literally crumbling away, the clay sliding into the water, the river mouth seeming to grow wider with each passing day.

Will's new wife was called Alice. She had skin that was quite transparent, the veins showing through, faintly, around her temples and on her neck. She'd been born in Illinois, but had moved to Salt Lake City with her father when she was thirteen. Why she had done this, and where the rest of her family was, remained a mystery. She answered questions with a listlessness that aroused an unnerving curiosity in Beth. It was as if words bored her, as if forming them with her tongue, moving them out through her lips, was somehow exhausting. It wasn't rudeness or shyness, Beth decided; it was something else.

Alice looked as if she had never seen a speck of sun, though her eyelashes were so fair they appeared to have been bleached by it. She had a long, slightly curved neck, and shoulders that sloped down to her arms. She looked to Will for answers, it seemed, which suited him just fine. She had left everything and everyone behind in America, and the thought of doing that, just for a man, made Beth feel like screaming. She said this to James, who was gay and single, and therefore, she thought, would acknowledge the foolishness of giving up one's life in this way, but he just ground his teeth at her when she said it, as if he had heard it all before.

Beth had met Alice the day before the registry office wedding. Will brought her round, unannounced and uninvited, at eight in the morning. Beth had just come inside from her five minutes of grass time. She was wearing her dressing gown and her hair was wild—finger-in-an-electric-socket wild. Funny that.

Will looked pleased with himself, but she didn't feel too pleased with him.

'Welcome back!' she said cheerily, trying desperately to tie her hair up into a bun.

He didn't go to hug her, but gestured to the side, elaborately, like a quiz-show host introducing a prize.

'This is Alice!' he said.

Alice smiled wanly and blinked her heavy, translucent eyelids, the veins under them glowing a soft lilac in the morning light. She tilted her head.

'Hello,' she said. She smiled more broadly once she had closed her mouth, but Beth noticed her fingers tapping against Will's left arm: tap-tap-tapping a Morse code, it seemed. *Save our souls. Save our souls.*

Indeed.

*

In America there was a hurricane—the worst, meteorologists said, in history.

It was curious, Beth thought, how everyone was willing to watch the news about that, how everyone wanted to talk about it, but not about the slow unravelling that was happening on home shores. The hurricane in America wrestled for first place in the media stakes, and won hands down. People switched their TV sets back on and sat in front of them, shaking their heads. Beth watched because of Alice, who had left America—her home—only two weeks before the storm hit, and who surely knew people affected.

There was endless home-video footage; one showing a freak wave rising over a road barrier, over the road, over a car with three shadowy figures inside, and then drawing itself back, sucking and sucking, so that when it was gone so too was the car, so too was the wheelie bin that had been blowing around on the pavement beside it, and there was only the jolting of the camera, an hysterical burble of words, the grey sea writhing away.

Beth went to the phone to call Will and Alice.

'I'm just ringing to see if Alice is okay,' she said to Will, who was breathing quietly down the line. There was a pause, a moment when neither of them spoke at all, and then Will cupped his hand over the receiver and Beth heard his voice, slightly muffled, calling out down the hallway.

'Are you okay,' he called out to Alice, 'about the hurricane and everything?'

Alice's voice seemed to slip through Will's fingers, seeping through the small plastic holes in the receiver like liquid. It seemed, by the time it reached Beth—sitting there on the couch in her living room—that it was hardly a voice at all, something more organic than that: water, perhaps, or air.

'Fine, thanks,' the voice replied, wearily.

'She's fine, thanks,' repeated Will directly down the line. He sounded relieved, really. Perhaps he hadn't asked her himself, perhaps he didn't know the answer. Beth didn't believe it anyway.

'Has she called home?' she said.

'Home?' Will took a bite of something and began to chew loudly. 'She never calls home.' There was a slap of a page being turned. Was he reading the paper?

'Well, I think that's odd,' said Beth. 'Don't you think that's odd?'

'She seems happy enough,' he said, sounding bored, vaguely irritated. He began to chew so audibly that Beth was certain the food couldn't be contained in his mouth.

'All right then,' she said. 'Have a good night,' and drew the conversation to a close.

*

In the paper there was a picture of more dead fish littered across the beach. They looked bloated and shiny, and lay belly up, facing the sky and the sun, as if that's where they'd come from; as if they'd fallen all that way before landing, stunned, on the sand. Some scientists said they suspected the growths were paralysing the fins so that the fish could no longer swim, and they simply rose to the surface of the water before being washed ashore.

The next day, though, when Beth looked in the paper for more news of the fish, there was no mention of them, or of the plague that was sweeping through the sea. That was yesterday's news. Instead, there was a three-page spread on the aftermath of the hurricane in America, with photos of human bodies that had been swept away and then brought back, fleshy and fat, waterlogged, bursting out of their clothes like sausages out of a skin.

It was certainly a season of bodies being gifted by the sea.

That weekend Will and Alice officially moved into the Landfall Motel. They had rented a unit there before actually taking ownership of it, since staying with Beth and Will's

parents—which they'd done, briefly, after their marriage—
had been unsurprisingly awkward, from all accounts. Will
had left home when he was sixteen, and a couple of years
later had moved to America like someone from an olden-
day film off to seek his fortune. He had not been back since,
although Beth's parents had been to visit him there once.
He seemed to be a stranger to them—a man who still
looked peculiarly boyish, his hands and feet too small and
pale-looking for a man of his size, a jaw that didn't have
the strength in it that the rest of his face seemed to require.
Even with his mouth closed, one of his front teeth forced
its way through, sitting on an angle against his bottom lip.
Beth noted all these things about him, feeling ashamed that
she could judge her own blood with the same distance, and
aloofness, that she might apply to a prospective boyfriend.
Perhaps she was just trying to understand things through
Alice's eyes. What do you *see* in him? was the question she
would have liked to put to her. What *is* it that you see?

On the day that Will and Alice took over the motel, Beth
and her parents went down there to look around. Will and
Alice were standing in reception, side by side, just waiting
for them, it seemed. Will had been talking to people in
town and had slowly but surely come to understand the
erosion problems on the river bank. He announced this to
them, once they were gathered around, with an authority
that suggested it was breaking news. He had clearly
forgotten that it was Beth and his parents who had first
tried to bring it to his attention. And now, of course, they
were all too kind to point this out to him. Tendons stood
out on his neck. Alice swallowed a lot, and loudly, as if she
were drinking air.

The two of them took Beth and her parents on a tour of the grounds, and the units, which ranged from *standard* to *deluxe*. Although Beth had driven past the motel many times, she had never been beyond its low concrete fence, and it felt strange stepping inside its walls, something so externally familiar but unknown. She looked around, feeling a little voyeuristic, at the wallpaper, the orange threadbare carpet, vinyl rising up behind the sink in the mini kitchens, the swimming pool with its film of green on the bottom.

'What's the difference between *standard* and *deluxe*?' asked their father, trying unsuccessfully not to sound critical or sarcastic.

Will drummed his fingertips against the back of Alice's neck, and cleared his throat.

'The *deluxe* units have a double and two single beds,' he said. 'Instead of bunks.'

'Oh, right,' said their father, and he nodded in an indulgent sort of way.

They continued on the tour, looking at the small creaky children's playground, the huddle of oaks by the laundry with picnic tables and chairs underneath. The oaks were covered in a thick froth of new leaves.

'It's really very nice,' said their mother to Will, and she smiled at him reassuringly.

'We'll turn it into the best motel in the southern hemisphere,' said Will, a brave trill in his voice. 'Won't we, Allie.'

She smiled mildly at them, at all of them, but didn't say a word.

As all five of them were sliding down the bank to look

at the river, Alice put her hand out to Beth—the first sign, really, that she wanted to know her—and turned her eyes towards her. In the grey afternoon her hair looked almost the same colour as her skin, washed out, a white gold with a throb of pink round the crown, the hint of scalp glowing through the roots. It was not Beth's mother she turned to—who really was slipping, and making a show of it—but Beth, who was managing fine. It seemed odd, this formal gentility, considering she was only three years older than Alice; they were peers. Beth felt a rush of sympathy for her, though sympathy seemed a cruel word.

'Don't let me shock you,' she said to Alice, thinking of the metal of Alice's wedding band, and the electric current pulsing in her own self, its fondness for anything metallic.

'Oh, you don't,' said Alice. She twisted her mouth as she said it, looking faintly mortified.

'I mean,' said Beth, 'give you a shock.'

Alice still didn't seem to understand. She stood staring at Beth quite blankly.

'I've been giving people shocks,' Beth said, beginning to feel exasperated. 'Electric ones.'

Alice still stared, though there seemed to be no judgment in her face. A breeze lifted her hair, showing the pink curl of her ears.

'Are you very tired?' she said to Beth.

'Yes,' Beth said. 'I guess, a little.'

Alice nodded and took back her hand—her hand which had remained extended the entire time—and slid it back into her jeans pocket. She nodded again, gravely, and turned away from Beth towards the water.

*

In the middle of that November Beth suddenly found she couldn't sleep. She went to bed every night dead beat, and lay there, blinking, into the early hours of the morning. She became obsessed with insomnia remedies, trying a new one each week. Baths with essential oils in them, counting sheep, chanting a self-affirming mantra for half an hour before bed.

'I will be able to sleep,' she said to herself and her bedroom walls over and over again. 'I *will* be able to sleep. I will be able to *sleep*.'

The more she wanted it, of course, the more elusive it became—something mysterious and fluid, sliding away from her whenever she got close. It reminded her, this feeling, of her relationships with men. How exhausting.

Sometimes she went outside, wondering if it was the static electricity that was causing her all this trouble and wanting to release it into the cracked earth. The sky seemed to be on her side once she was out there, curving over her like an enormous hood, caring and yet uncaring, like God. It would be there regardless, no matter how bad things got; no matter if her chest opened like a door and her organs fell out, landing at her feet in a jumble. *No matter. No matter*—when nothing is left, it isn't important any more.

It was on one of these nights that the phone rang at half-past eleven, long after Beth had gone to bed. It rang three times and then stopped, and then rang again, and she clambered out of her sheets in the dark.

The voice on the other end of the line didn't say hello, or sorry, but paused just after Beth picked up.

'I wasn't sure if you'd still be awake,' it said, 'I didn't know if I should try.' And then there was silence for what felt like minutes.

Beth didn't instantly recognise the voice, though she should have, considering the soft soap-opera lilt. She squinted into the dark and rubbed her forehead.

'I'm sorry?' she said.

'*Did* I wake you?' said the voice.

Beth squinted harder, and then realised. It was Alice. She had never rung before.

'Is there something wrong?' Beth said.

'No, no.' She paused, but didn't sound certain. 'I just thought you might like to see it. What's happening down here.' And then she paused again. 'Will's asleep,' she said emphatically.

Beth felt seized by a strange anxiety, her heart pounding somewhere near her throat. *Was* there something wrong?

'I'll be there right away,' she said to Alice, and slammed the receiver back into place.

Beth got down to the Landfall Motel just fifteen minutes after Alice had called. She had put a sweatshirt on over her pyjama top, but was still wearing the bottoms—adorned with skiing penguins—and running shoes with no socks. She hardly remembered driving there, and felt appallingly rattled, as if she was about to walk in on a crime scene; find her brother, throat slit, in the bath.

Alice was waiting for her outside the reception area. She was wearing a light windbreaker, the hood pulled up over her head. She moved towards the headlights like someone in a dream, her face white and eyes wide.

She stood waiting while Beth tumbled her jelly limbs out the car door.

'You were very quick,' she said then. 'You weren't asleep, were you? Not with your insomnia?'

'What's happened?' Beth said, moving jerkily towards her across the gravel. 'Is it Will, Alice? What's happened?'

Alice looked taken aback. She pulled the hood off her head, and her hair seemed to light up the car park, pulsing slightly in its whiteness like a light bulb.

'Will's asleep,' she said calmly. 'I told you that.'

'I just thought . . .' said Beth, and then stammered to a halt.

'Will's asleep,' said Alice again.

Beth faced her, breathing hard. 'I was so worried,' she said. She felt as if her voice would crack.

Alice didn't seem to understand. Her face was blank. Did she not know that it was she who had caused this chaos inside Beth's head?

'I thought you'd be awake too,' she said. 'I just thought you'd be awake.'

Beth nodded.

'I was.'

This affirmation seemed to make Alice brighten, though only in a small way.

'When I saw it I thought of you instantly,' she said, and she smiled, showing her teeth. 'I had to look everywhere for your number. But I really thought I should call. You'd want to see this, I thought. You and the electricity.'

Beth rubbed her forehead. It seemed Alice was speaking

in some kind of riddle; she couldn't quite grasp the words.

'Let's go,' said Alice, and she turned and started walking down towards the river.

Beth had a mini torch on the key ring her father had given her in case of emergencies. She turned it on now and moved towards Alice, having to jog a little to catch up. The leaves of the trees rustled around her. One of the units had lights on and the curtains closed. As they walked past, she heard the sound of men's voices, slightly raised, drunk possibly. Alice sped up and flicked the hood of her jacket over her head, holding it in place tight under her chin with one hand.

'I thought of you,' she said again.

Beth could already see what it was before they got there, even though she was a little distance away on the bank. She followed Alice down, so that her toes were perched right on the edge.

Alice turned her eyes towards her then.

'Isn't it like electricity?' she said.

That feeling—of something magical—crept towards Beth, filling her up so that she too suddenly felt truly alive.

'Yes,' she said. 'It is.'

The water was on fire, or that's how it seemed. It was lit up like a Christmas tree, or fireworks in a night sky. It was as if tiny stars had fallen down and were moving around in there, under the surface.

'I've never seen it before,' said Alice. 'Is it phosphorescence? Is that what it's called?'

Beth had seen it, though not for years, and never like this. She pulled the bulkiness of her sweatshirt around herself, feeling where the air was getting in, and moved her feet up and down in small jogging steps to keep warm. Little balls of clay rolled out of the bank under her feet, dropping almost soundlessly into the river.

'It's beautiful,' she said to Alice. 'Thank you for calling me, it's beautiful.'

Alice didn't turn to her, or smile, but she reached out her fingers and found Beth's wrist, clamped her hand around it. Her fingers felt cool and smooth and finely made, the bones under the skin fragile as china. She just held on to Beth, quite tight, so that the blood in her wrist began to drum loudly against the skin.

'You know the electricity you get,' she said to Beth, 'and the shocks? You know how you were telling me? I've got something in my throat,' she said. 'It's been here for weeks, the feeling. Like a bone is stuck in there—' she moved her free hand up towards her neck, and swept her fingernail across it in a dramatic slitting gesture— 'lying right across it,' she said. 'Like that.'

There was a sound behind them, though Beth hardly registered it. It seemed heavy and yet quiet, somehow; a shuffling, a rustling under the ground and on top of it; something natural and normal, wind or water. Neither Beth nor Alice turned to see what it was.

'Is there something wrong?' said Beth. 'You must miss your family.'

'Who knows?' said Alice lightly. 'There's only him.' She moved her lips over her teeth and bit into them. 'I wouldn't miss *him*,' she said.

'Your father?'

Alice may have shrugged her shoulder slightly. Beth couldn't tell. She had let go of Beth's wrist now, but her arm still seemed to be outstretched towards her, as if she was feeling her way in the dark.

'Are things all right with Will?' said Beth. 'Alice?'

Alice tilted her head, and stared out across the river at the bank on the other side, the dark swarm of trees on its edge, the road beyond them. The headlights of a car swung into view, lighting up the trees, shocking their leaves into life. Even though the car was some distance away, the sound of its engine and its tyres against the road soared towards them, a rushing hiss that snapped off as the car swung away into the black.

Perhaps it was that—the suddenness of the car, close and yet far away—that made Beth turn around, the shell of quiet having been broken. She did not just move her head, but her whole body, and she found herself facing Will, who was standing behind them, a few metres away, his hands shoved deep into the pockets of his dressing gown. She heard a sound come out of her own mouth like the faint cry of a bird.

Alice didn't move, her face staring straight ahead out across the water.

'Will,' Alice said, without hesitation or alarm, but still quite loudly. She had not turned to see him, but she knew, somehow, he was there.

Will was only wearing his boxer shorts, the dressing gown open, flapping slightly against his legs. The lamps on the porch of the laundry were on, and they glowed behind him so that he looked like a cut-out, his hair on a sharp triangular angle, set like that from sleep. Beth didn't know what to say.

She tried to smile.

'Hi,' she said. 'You're awake.'

He lifted his hands to his face and seemed almost to claw at it, rubbing at his eyes and eyebrows.

'And you are too,' he said to Beth. 'Or are you? Awake? What are you doing out here? What are you two doing out here together?'

Despite his agitation, Alice remained quite still, her arms by her sides.

'Beth and I are just looking at things,' she said calmly.

He made a coughing sound. 'Looking at things?'

'Looking at things.' Her tone was firm, as if she were a teacher, he the child.

She turned suddenly towards him, so that the three of them were placed like points of a triangle.

Will started to laugh, though it was a vaguely hysterical sound.

'Beth,' he said. 'What on *earth* is going on?'

Beth could feel Alice's breathing beside her, the soft snuffle of it—in and out—rapid but not strained. She had lifted her hand to her throat and was holding it there against the skin.

Will, always prone to tantrums, lifted one bare foot up and then pounded it against the ground, making the whole bank quake.

'Could someone tell me what is going on?' he said, and then swallowed hard. 'Come back to bed,' he said, far too angrily. 'I don't know what the hell is going on out here, but I'm asking you, Allie. Please. Come back to bed.'

His shoulders seemed to collapse forward, and for a moment Beth thought he might cry.

'She only called me because of the electricity,' Beth said, 'and the river. It's nothing to worry about, Will. Come on now. Quieten down.'

'Come back to bed,' he said to Alice again, though he was looking at his feet.

'No thank you,' she said sweetly, her eyes wide, her hand still held to her throat. 'I like it out here at the moment,' and she smiled at him encouragingly.

Will let out an exasperated shuddering sigh, and flapped his arms around a little, and looked from Alice to Beth and back again.

'This has to stop,' he said to Alice. 'Why can't you just stay in bed at night? Like normal people.'

If he wanted an answer, he didn't wait for it. He seemed to pick himself up—pulling his shoulders back, lifting his head—and without another word turned and walked away from them, the dressing gown flying out behind him like a cloak.

Alice continued to smile, watching him go.

'Is there something wrong between you two?' Beth said, but Alice paid no attention. She turned back towards the river as if she had simply erased Will with one blink. She looked into the water for a moment, and then she moved her fingers towards Beth's arm, took hold of her wrist again.

'Do you think you could look for me?' she said. 'In my throat? With your torch?'

Beth didn't know what to say. She felt slightly embarrassed, and overtired—as if she could cry. She looked at the darting lights in the water.

'Okay,' she said, and then she paused. 'Of course.'

Alice moved her head immediately towards her, holding her wrist tight, and opened her mouth wide. The breeze lifted her hair again, like it had when she had reached out her hand to Beth on the bank. It looked so thin and light, as if it could lift off her head and float away.

Beth turned on the torch and shone it right down Alice's throat. The pinkness, rawness, of it jumped towards her. She could smell the slight sourness of Alice's breath, like something that had once been sweet but wasn't any more: milk on the turn. Her epiglottis jolted around nervously, but other than that nothing seemed unusual. It was just raw-looking and ridgy, like all throats, Beth imagined.

'I don't think I'm going to be able to see anything,' she said, straining her neck, bobbing her eyes around. 'I can't tell. I don't think I can see far enough down.'

Alice dropped her head, and shut her mouth, and swallowed hard.

'I don't think it is a bone,' she said. 'I don't think there's anything stuck. It's just the feeling.'

And then she smiled, quite brightly. 'Thanks for looking anyway,' she said. She released her grip on Beth's wrist, and leaned her head back so she was looking at the sky. She lifted her arms out to her sides.

'It's probably nothing to worry about,' she said. 'Thanks all the same.'

The wind stirred the trees again, and the water, so that the surface rippled. Beth swung her head back so she too was looking at the sky.

'What do you think's up there?' said Alice, and she

flapped her arms slightly. 'I think a whole lot of nothing,' she said. She seemed lighter, and whiter—if that was possible; as if she had unloaded a great weight.

A whole lot of nothing. *No matter. No matter.*

Beth turned to look at her. 'Maybe that and something else, too,' she said.

Alice didn't say anything, but Beth felt her silent agreement. The outline of her profile was tilted right back, so that her neck seemed to form a straight line right up to her chin.

'I'm glad you called,' Beth said, and Alice nodded, a blurry movement, a flash of white in the dark.

'Yes,' she said definitely, the word moving out of her mouth and into the night. 'Yes.'

Beth just stood there looking at Alice, and Alice looked up, directing her words at nothing in particular.

'Do you ever get the feeling that there's nowhere left to go?' she said, though she didn't wait for Beth's answer. 'Like you're all locked up, but as soon as you're set free you just stand there waiting to be let back in. And it isn't even that it's a bone,' she said again. 'I'm pretty sure of that. But sometimes I feel as if I could hook my finger down and pull one out.' She scuffed her feet against the ground. 'I'd like the feeling,' she said, 'of pulling something out of there.' She smiled then to herself, a faint curl of her lips, still looking up at the sky, blinking hard.

'How does it feel right now?' Beth said.

'Okay,' said Alice. 'Okay, thanks.' And then she paused. 'Thanks for coming,' she said, and paused again. 'Beth.'

The breeze rose again, out of nowhere, lifting a plastic bag off the bank, making it roll across the grass, crackling and cackling. The hood of Alice's jacket flapped against her back, filling with air so that, for a moment, it looked quite round and solid. In the distance Beth could hear voices, though they seemed very far away. Alice's head was still craned back, and her mouth slightly open, showing the edge of her straight white teeth.

'Look at them,' said Alice. 'All those stars.'

And Beth did, tilting her head right back again. It was true. There were so many of them, blinking in the sky, scattered across it in clusters. They seemed reflected in the water too, alive in there, moving around.

'And the moon,' said Alice. 'So white!'

She said it with great emphasis—*so white*—and it occurred to Beth that she could just as well be talking about herself. *So white!* She felt a rush of relief—was that what it was?—move out from her chest, right down to her fingertips. *No matter. No matter*—even that everything was falling apart. There were stars all around them, in the waters at their feet, high above their heads, and the moon seemed just to have been thrown in for good measure. It was new—the moon—so slim and pale, and it looked quite out of place amongst the stars, like a shard of bone half eaten away.

Michael's Fasting
for Christmas

It was the third most traumatic experience in your life. That's what Amy read in a magazine. Coming in, in third place after death and divorce—bronze medal, not a winner but not a loser either—was moving house. Such an ordinary, everyday experience, but there it was, in the top three. Amy wondered if they had asked the Africans. Did this survey include the Africans too? She thought a lot about them these days. Not as much as when she was a kid and her mother used them as an example for why she should eat all her dinner, and also for why she couldn't have ice cream for afternoon tea, but quite a lot all the same. Do the *African* children have ice cream? Amy's mother used to say to her, knowing full well that she knew the answer. Maybe all the guilt had got into her head like some poor soggy Catholic.

Anyway, being starving but still alive was probably more traumatic than moving house. If Amy could find out who had conducted the survey, she would send that to them in a letter. She could get it printed on a teeshirt. She could start a campaign. She thought about it all afternoon, and then she realised something. She couldn't do any of these things; she couldn't because she was just as bad as the rest; she couldn't because at the moment when she read the statistic, standing in the checkout queue in the supermarket, she had thought to herself, No. No, she had thought, Christmas should be there in third place. Just like the true middle-class girl she was, she had thought instantly of trauma and Christmas.

She had remembered the Africans later.

That was the year that Michael fasted. That's probably why it was on Amy's mind, Christmas that is, because it was the 22nd of December; the countdown was well underway. The next day her mother called her at work, on the direct line that was reserved for emergencies. That's what Amy told her, anyway.

'Well, he's fasting,' she said. No hello, how are you. No explanation, just straight in there, as if she was picking up on a conversation that had been left off mid-thread.

Amy was sorting the papers on her desk into piles, most important to least. She bit at her fingernail.

'Sorry?'

'Michael,' her mother said definitively. 'He's fasting. For Christmas.'

There was a pregnant pause, and Amy heard a little puff of breath coming down the phone line. She felt as if it could hit her in the ear, like spit.

'What do you mean he's fasting?'

'He's fasting,' her mother said again. 'Some health kick. It's a ten-day one, and he says he won't stop, not even for Christmas dinner. Meredith called me in tears.'

Meredith was Amy's oldest sister. She got weepy a lot. It was her allergies, apparently.

Amy let out a cynical snort and leaned back in her chair.

'Well, I think that's hilarious,' she said.

'Hilarious?' her mother said. 'The Stroms are coming this year, and Grandma and Grandpop. Hilarious? Amy, you really do have a warped sense of humour.' Her voice quavered a little as she said it, but not in an irritable way; she sounded almost admiring.

'Maybe he's trying to be Christ,' Amy said, chewing on her fingernails, staring absent-mindedly out the window.

'Trying to be *nice*?' her mother said. 'Oh, I don't think so.'

'No—Christ.'

'Oh, *Christ*,' her mother said wistfully, suddenly calm, disinterested, the excitement of the gossip seeming to have drained her. 'Yes, maybe.'

*

Meredith had met Michael six months after her divorce from Jeff (life trauma no. 2, according to the *New Woman* magazine).

She had started seeing him almost immediately.

He took such good *care* of himself, she told Amy once, and when she said it Amy imagined a man who wore beige pants and boat shoes and washed his hands with a fragrant moisturising soap. That wasn't what Michael was at all; that wasn't quite the care Meredith had been talking about. It was more an inner sort of cleanliness that he was into, polishing organs instead of shoes, that sort of thing.

He owned a Water Alkaliser that had cost a thousand dollars, and a juicer that swallowed lemons whole, transforming them into a milky liquid that was as good as doing a six-week liver cleanse, according to Michael. Meredith, who was only thirty-two, but who had somehow started to lose her lustre, took on a certain pre-pubescent glow once he started feeding her his concoctions. Amy's mother noticed it too, but put it down to new love, or something. After Jeff, she said, any man with hairs on his chest would do the trick, no matter who he was or what he was into. Amy was inclined to agree, about Jeff anyway, but she didn't know if love had ever improved *her* skin that much. She even got Meredith to send her a pamphlet on Colloidal Silver, which was the latest advance in health technology, apparently.

The peculiar thing was that despite all the inner vacuuming Michael did, he didn't look that much the better for it. He was a good ten years older than Meredith, and maybe compared to other forty-somethings he was doing okay, but there was something about him that wasn't quite right. His skin had a yellowish tinge, like he was always standing under fluorescent lights, and it seemed to be pulled tight across his shaved head: tight as a drum, almost parched, like the skin of a mummy.

When Amy said that to her mother, she'd taken it quite the wrong way.

'Well motherhood is very *hard*,' she'd said, 'but considering that I've probably lost my looks for you, I don't think you should go around shouting the fact from the rooftops.'

'No,' Amy said. 'A *mummy*. A dead one.'

'Oh,' her mother said, 'those.'

*

The drive from Amy's house to her parents' took an hour and a half. They had wanted her to go up on Christmas Eve so they could do stockings on the end of the bed, just like when she was small, but she said no, using the traffic as a suitably safety-conscious excuse.

Ben had flown out at 11 p.m. on Christmas Eve. His family liked to celebrate Christmas at different geographical sites each year. For the last one they'd gone to some mountain on the Volcanic Plateau, and worn Santa hats on the tramp up there. There was a photo of them all garbed up, eating turkey sandwiches, sitting cross-legged around a gingham cloth spread across the dust. This year they were going to a lake, were going to have smoked trout and pavlova out of a chilly bin, sitting right out in the middle of the water in a family friend's boat.

Ben tried to pretend it wasn't fun, for her sake.

'Have a Merry Christmas,' he'd said to her, standing in the wind outside the airport, holding her hand in a non-committal way.

'Yeah,' Amy said brightly. 'You too.'

He tried to smile as if he wouldn't. Whatever.

Amy had a piece of toast for breakfast, and packed her bags, and set off just after nine. She listened to talkback radio to avoid the hymns.

'Mer-ry Christmas!' the host kept hollering every time a new caller came through. One woman, her words slurring slightly, said she was going to be celebrating with her dear friend Gypsy, which sounded fine until she let slip that Gypsy was her cat. At that point Amy turned the radio off and sang 'O Tannenbaum'—which they'd learned in German at school—just to see if she could remember the words. She was okay on the chorus, but the verses, she discovered, required a certain amount of concentration.

She pulled into her parents' drive just after eleven. Her mother's wide white face appeared in the kitchen window. She came hoppity-hopping out the back door.

'You made it here in one piece!' she said tremulously, as if it was one of the great miracles of modern-day life.

Which it was, really, if you thought about it.

Meredith and Michael, and Howard and Ann Strom, and their friend Bill, and Amy's father were all sitting in the living room.

'Here she is!' Amy's father said. He had a paper crown on his head, and little tufts of hair poked out the top and sides, seeming quite out of place and odd, like the hair on a hippopotamus. The couch seemed to be in the process of swallowing him whole, sucking his small soft body down, down into its stuffing.

He looked remarkably cheery for a man about to disappear.

'This is our Amy,' he said to the room, even though everyone there had met her before.

They nodded and shuffled, Meredith launching herself out of her armchair and duck-footing it over to Amy to give her a wet kiss on the cheek; Michael getting in the queue behind her; Amy's father and the Stroms heaving themselves off the couch. They all lined up, like children waiting to have their photo with Father Christmas.

'Merry Christmas!' Amy said to each one of them.

Really, all she needed was a beard.

At 11.30 her grandparents arrived, which was always a miracle—they were in their nineties and still believed they could drive—and the line-up re-formed, with Amy a part of it this time, standing at the back next to Howard Halitosis Strom, who asked her for the second time what it was she was doing with her life these days. For the second time that day she tried to use diversion tactics to avoid admitting that she spent eight hours a day sitting at a desk doing next to nothing. Howard smiled. He wasn't the least bit interested in the answer anyway.

'And your father tells me,' he said, aiming the words moistly at her left cheek, 'that Zoë is doing extremely well.'

This was the conversation he really wanted to have. He just had to get past the preliminaries first.

'Yes,' said Amy, smiling cheerily back, 'she is.'

'How splendid,' said Howard. And then he was washed away on the hellos.

This is how it would go, this Christmas like any other: Amy fielding questions about Zoë who probably wouldn't have managed to field them all on her own, even if she'd been there. Zoë was the middle sister, and because she was closer in age and looks to Amy, it was Amy, not Meredith, whom everyone went to for information.

She was trying her luck in London, after spending four years on a soap in Australia. There had been an article on her in *Woman's Day*. There were whole websites dedicated to the death of her character, Lydia Ford, killed off in a car accident. Zoë had recently got her first role in the UK, playing a young sassy mother in a VW Beetle advertisement. There was a certain irony in this, Amy thought, considering what a car had done to poor Lydia Ford.

Did anyone else see the irony in this?

She didn't like to bring it up for fear of sounding spiteful.

Which she wasn't. Spiteful, that is. It was just that the same conversation got wheeled out over and over again, like a gelatinous stew on a hospital tray. Two years ago, at a family reunion, distant relative after distant relative had launched their quivering selves towards her, believing her to be the shining star. She had politely pointed each one of them in the right direction, over by the presents pile, or the punch bowl, and off they'd gone, unashamedly, as if they were disciples on a pilgrimage to Mecca. As the night wore on, and it certainly did just that, Amy's patience began to wear a little thin as well.

'So are *you* the actress?' a boggly-eyed old trout asked as Amy tried to slip outside for some air.

'No,' said Amy, 'I'm the stripper.'

'Right,' the woman said, 'I mean wrong—wrong one.' And she opened and shut her small round fishy mouth and swallowed twice—glug, glug—like there was something stuck there in her throat.

'I can see that now, actually,' she said. 'Now that I'm up close.' She tapped at Amy's arm with her fingers, trying to be affectionate but actually pushing her away, and scooted back inside.

'So are you the *piranha*?' Amy called after her, once the door had swung back into place. She called it, but it was under her breath really.

Bad move, nonetheless.

Christmas dinner was scheduled for one o'clock, but first they had to put on hats to make it feel like a celebration. Amy's father was leading the way in that regard; he'd been wearing his, apparently, since 10 a.m. He was decreasing in age, it seemed; was sweeter and odder every time Amy saw him. She expected, come Easter, for him to be wearing school socks and a blazer; nappies the Christmas after that.

'It covers up my bald patches,' he said to her jollily, unfolding a paper hat for her—a green one, because he knew it was her favourite colour. 'And it pins my ears back.'

'Do you think it can cover my face?' Amy said.

'What would you want to do *that* for?' he said in a tone only a parent could use.

She pulled the crinkled paper down over her hair and head—hard, so that it ripped. She hadn't meant for that to happen. It came away in her hands, a flaccid strip of tissue.

Without a word, her father trotted off to the kitchen to get her another.

Amy's grandparents, Grandma and Grandpop, perched side by side on the couch, their hands in their laps, were already wearing theirs. They were still snipping at each other, quietly, about Grandpop's failure to brake fast enough at the zebra crossing.

'They hadn't even stepped out onto the road, *love*,' he hissed, aiming the words out the corner of his mouth.

'Yes, dear,' she replied. 'So you keep saying. But some-times, you know, people *speed up*.' She blinked rapidly as she said the last two words, demonstrating the acceleration, it seemed, with her lids.

Howard Strom was sitting in the armchair over by the window.

'So, your granddaughter Zoë,' he said, 'is making it big in London, I hear.'

'Sorry, dear?' Amy's Grandma leaned forward in her chair, clasping her hands tighter in her lap. Being hard of hearing ran in the family. Like mother, like daughter, Amy thought, and then realised that if they were like that she probably would be one day too.

'Your granddaughter!' he shouted. 'Mak-ing it Big! In London!'

'Oh yes,' Grandma said, 'but she isn't here today—' and then she paused, uncertain in her certainty— 'is she?'

In the kitchen, Meredith and Amy's mother were making preparations for the feast. Meredith had developed a brusqueness of movement she brought out just on family occasions, just around their mother. It was an 'everything is under control' quality—slightly tight lipped—which was amusing considering she only wore Indian cotton, and as a result looked floaty and ethereal, at first glance. Amy's mother was seeing to the turkey, and Meredith was vigorously chopping parsley, the knife rattling against the board. She'd whipped her dark, fuzzy hair into a ponytail on the top of her head, and each curly strand shimmied with her movement.

'Now Michael will have a *little* bit of turkey, won't he?' said Amy's mother, fowl fat up to her wrists.

'I've already told you, Mum,' Meredith said. 'You know the answer.'

'A little bit can't hurt, surely.'

Meredith ground one toe against the lino and scratched her head.

'He might have a couple of Dad's sugar snap peas,' she said.

'Well, what's the difference then? Peas? Turkey? They both go in your mouth.'

'He'd only do it so he'd have something to put on his plate.' She bit her at her lip and raised her eyes to the ceiling in an exaggerated Don't Cry display.

'Jesus wept,' said Amy's mother.

'Well, don't make me weep too.'

Amy moved into the kitchen between them, suddenly aware of the knife in Meredith's hand and her seemingly frayed nerves.

'Maybe we could put him on the table as a centrepiece,' she said. She was trying to be light. 'We could put a glaze on him. He could meditate.'

She spotted Michael out the kitchen window then, down by the back fence, hovering around the vegetable garden. His lanky frame was stooped, the shoulders rolling forward slightly towards his chest, his oval head glowing in the midday light.

'Goodness, Amy!' said her mother. That appalled quaver again, with the undertone of delight. 'What a sense of humour!' And she lifted the slippery bird up out of its baking dish and dropped it heavily onto an enormous plate. It slid out of her hands, looking for a moment like a soaped-up baby, skating helplessly under the water in a bath.

Amy's father came into the kitchen and grabbed another paper crown out of the packet.

'I'll take this out to Michael,' he said to Meredith, patting her supportively on the back. 'Just because he isn't eating, doesn't mean he can't join in on the fun now, does it?'

He headed off to the vegetable patch, putting on a Christmas carols CD on his way out the door.

Amy went to get the champagne glasses from the cabinet. Grandma and Grandpop were still in the living room, trying to have a conversation with the Stroms' friend Bill, who was trying to have a conversation with them back. Neither party was having much success. Howard was studying the family photos on the bookcase;

Ann was setting the table. It seemed that everyone was waiting for something to happen. Perhaps just for the food. Amy headed back into the kitchen and finished her job, mixing the last of the cream into the trifle.

'What about a little glass of sherry,' Amy's mother said to Meredith, 'just a little one? For Michael?'

Meredith said, 'Mum,' which really meant no.

At 1.15—a little behind schedule—they all gathered around the dining-room table, and spread their Christmas napkins on their laps, and adjusted their party hats.

Amy's father turned down the music, just a touch.

'Well, Happy Christmas everyone,' said Amy's mother, and they all started to eat. All of them, that is, except for Michael, who took small sips of his glass of water, and every now and then looked at his plate—large, white, empty, apart from four pea pods, still with their stalks—almost wonderingly.

'Aren't you having any turkey, old chap?' said Howard Strom, chewing on a crisp piece of skin as he spoke.

The rings under Michael's eyes seemed to grow darker.

'Oh no thanks,' he said, as brightly as he could.

'Some roast vegetables?' said Howard, clearly not getting the message, behaving as if it was his house, as if he was the host.

'No thanks,' said Michael.

Meredith stuck a large piece of potato in her mouth, but didn't start chewing it. She stared, instead, at her quivering fork.

'Well, what about some more greens then?' said Howard. Was he drunk?

Amy's father looked at her, and looked at the table cloth, and then at the wall. Finally he looked at Howard.

'Michael is fasting,' he said, with more assertiveness than Amy thought she had ever heard him use in her life.

Amy's mother cleared her throat and patted at her hair.

'On Christmas Day?' said Howard.

'On Christmas Day,' said Amy's father, and he smiled at Michael as if to say, Never mind, boy, eat your peas.

'Fasting on Christmas Day,' repeated Howard. 'Did you hear that, Ann?'

His wife nodded.

'Well I'll be damned,' he said.

Amy felt a banging in her head, as if there was a small angry thing in there trying to get out. She looked at Howard's thick fat neck, the jowls hanging in flaps just below his jaw line. He stuffed another enormous piece of turkey into his mouth.

'In the West,' she said to him, 'we eat far more than we actually need.'

Her voice trembled a little as she said it. Had she read that somewhere, or was she simply making it up? She would carry on regardless. She thought of the African children, their limbs like sticks, their bellies round and empty as coconuts. This speech was for them. For them, and for Michael, who just happened to be the underdog today.

'We're greedy,' she said, meaning, you, Howard. 'In a village in Japan people live well into their hundreds, and they say it's because they only eat as much as they need, not as much as they want.'

Where had that come from? Was it true?

Howard continued to chew on his flap of turkey, and then swallowed, watching Amy the whole time.

'Well, I say if you've got it, flaunt it,' he said. 'No use in cutting down on a bit of pleasure just for the sake of it now, is there?'

If Amy had been ten, she would have said to herself, or her mother, or whoever was speaking, 'Why don't I put my dinner in an envelope and mail it to the starving children then? They can have it.' She would have said that. She would have agreed with Howard. No use in cutting down just for the sake of it, is there? Just because they're starving doesn't mean we should too. She was going round in circles, like a dog chasing its tail. She was turning into her mother.

'The saying, If you've got it, flaunt it, is about good looks,' she said to Howard. 'Not about food.' She smiled at him then, attempting to soften the blow. She was skating off into the middle of a frozen lake, and the ice was going to crack any second.

'Is she saying I'm not a good-looking man?' guffawed Howard.

Meredith looked at Amy, the whites showing all the way round her eyes. Her eyes were fair anyway, a pale eggshell blue, and at that moment their blueness seemed to be fading into the white of her face. When she was young, Meredith had always lacked the effortless glamour of her high school friends—all of whom seemed unbearably glamorous to Amy and Zoë. She had lacked a certain sheen, and this bothered them, both of them—perhaps all of them?—though no one ever let on. If her two younger sisters were trying to follow in her footsteps in that regard, she had sure tried to lead them up the garden path. But sitting there, right across from her, so wild and so white, Amy felt a surge of fondness for Meredith who had always been there in her life, coveted or not. At that moment she looked a little like a reptile, her washed-out face bordered by a flush of red that was creeping in large circular patches up her neck. She was going to attempt to rescue her—to rescue the rescuer. Amy could feel it.

'Michael has been unwell,' Meredith said, quite loudly, and the flush on her neck seemed to fade, almost immediately. 'He's trying to get rid of his toxicity.'

Amy's father nodded at her, as if to say, That's right. A strange hush had fallen on the table. Amy realised that the Christmas CD had stopped. It was drizzling outside. Her mother was chewing sombrely on a piece of boiled carrot, her arms slack by her side. Down the end of the table Grandma and Grandpop, blissfully unaware of the discomfort around them, were simultaneously cutting at something on their plates. They were simply two halves of one thing, each side doing its job. Michael picked up one podded pea and held it between his fingertips.

'What sort of unwell has he been?' said Howard to Meredith, as if Michael was not in the room.

'Honestly Howard!' said Ann.

'Well I'm only asking.'

Amy looked to her mother, who looked at Meredith, who looked at Michael. He nodded at her, but looked into his plate.

'Cancer!' said Meredith, with more force than she needed to.

Amy's mother let out a half-muffled cry. Ann lifted her hands to the base of her throat. The skin on Meredith's face suddenly seemed to be pulled tight back, back towards her hairline. 'Cancer,' she said again, 'and he cured himself, I'll have you know! Michael is a brave man. He needs to watch his toxicity.'

And then she burst into tears.

'Did-You-Know-About-This?' Amy's mother mouthed to her across the table. Amy shook her head. She looked at Meredith who was dabbing at her face with her Christmas napkin, and at Michael who was holding her hand. She realised what it was about him that she had found odd all along. He looked defeated, like a man whose car had broken down in the middle of a desert. In this case, though, the car was his own body: engine trouble once; perhaps nothing more than a flat tyre now. He was a man surrounded by car-repairing apparatus and yet his car was causing him trouble, cleansing machines and all.

'You never told us,' said Amy's mother quietly.

'Well, you'd all *worry*,' said Meredith. 'Wouldn't you?'

'Well I'll be damned,' said Howard Strom again.

For a moment nobody said anything else.

Outside—somewhere over the fence—children were singing Christmas carols. Michael cleared his throat and tried to smile.

'If you don't have your health, you don't have anything,' he said brightly.

'Quite right!' said Amy's father, and he picked up his glass. 'Let's drink to that!' He stumbled to his feet, and so did the rest of them, Michael lagging behind a bit, Amy's grandparents also, so that it looked for a moment as if they were raising a toast to the three of them, still partially seated, partially airborne.

'If you don't have your health, you don't have anything!' said Amy's father.

'If you don't have your *what,* dear?' said Grandma.

'If you don't have your hearing,' Howard Strom said to her, 'you don't have anything!' Clearly he was making a last-ditch attempt at joke of the day. He laughed at himself, but no one laughed with him.

'Oh, indeed,' said Amy's Grandmother. 'But at least we've got each other.' She smiled almost smugly then, though not at Grandpop, even though the smile was certainly meant for him.

Outside, the sound of carols grew louder, a wordless, jolly sound, almost like birds. Were they coming closer, the carol singers? Amy's father heard them too.

'Listen to that!' he said, as if he had organised the musical interlude himself. 'Merry Christmas, everyone.'

Amy's mother made a sound of agreement in her throat, but she looked about as merry as someone who'd been hit on the head with a frying pan.

They all sat back down again, scraping their chairs against the floor, their glasses clinking a little as they found their places. Grandma and Grandpop were the only ones left standing—still holding their glasses out in front of them, not ready to let gravity push their creaky joints back into their seats. They both looked out the window at the rain.

'Do you think they've made trifle again this year?' said

Grandpop out the corner of his mouth, unaware that the whole table was his audience.

Grandma blinked chirpily, her milky blue eyes staring out the window as if she was waiting for a colourful bird, an angel perhaps, to descend from the sky.

'Oh I hope so!' she said, with such vigour it was as if she had more life left in her than all ten of them combined.

*

The Stroms left earlier than usual, taking their friend Bill with them. In previous years they had stayed until it was dark, to watch the Queen's Christmas message broadcast on TV. This, it had always seemed, was Howard's favourite part of the day, when he could make the same jokes about the corgis, and the corgis and Prince Phillip, and the corgis and Prince Phillip and the Queen. Ann and Amy's parents, and whoever else was pretending to pay attention, would make a show of being amused and horrified, which was the required reaction. Their performance—this unwavering ability to hold up their side of the bargain— was the most impressive performance of all. But this year no one, including Howard, seemed to have the stomach for it, not even for the evening news.

'This was the nicest Christmas I've ever had,' said Bill as they were getting ready to leave. He had a limp that seemed to have been acquired recently, sometime between Christmas dinner and dessert. Was he being polite or trying to be funny? No one could tell, and so no one responded or even acknowledged his statement. He announced it to the room, and the room wouldn't hear it. His limp was the only thing that made him seem crestfallen—and the limp, surely, was to do with a bad hip or displaced joint. He continued to smile, though, following Ann and Howard all the way down the hall, smiling all the time.

'That really was a nice Christmas,' he said again once they'd reached the front door.

'Wasn't it?' said Amy's mother, trying to smile back, though she narrowed her eyes as she said it—perhaps in disbelief.

'Come along, Bill!' Ann called to him, and just like a dog, or a badly shaped horse, he began to trot along towards the car in a lopsided canter, still favouring his left leg.

'What a lovely day!' they all called to each other, from a safe distance.

'Bye bye! Thank you! Great day!'

'Bye! Great day!'

To Amy's ears—though perhaps delirium was simply setting in—it sounded like something else entirely. Hate day! Hate day! Everyone waving and smiling and the truth was slipping out of their mouths in disguise.

Grandma and Grandpop, standing at the back of the huddle by the front door, waved too, though seemingly at each other.

Amy's mother closed the front door.

'Well!' she said. And she turned back towards the rest of the group. Nobody else moved. They all stood there. Amy's parents, and Meredith and Michael and Grandma and Grandpop and Amy herself. The top button of Amy's mother's dress had come undone, possibly during the exertion of the waving and goodbyes. She looked as though she'd just been caught in a gust of wind or, even worse, some kind of appallingly passionate sexual encounter.

'Well,' she said again, but with less purpose this time.

They all looked at the floor, or the walls, but not at each other.

'That might have been my last Christmas,' said Grandma suddenly, a defiant edge in her voice. 'At my age you start thinking things like that.'

Amy's mother started to laugh, but then stopped herself. Perhaps she knew what was coming next.

'Mine too,' said Michael. 'I think that too.' And then he paused and smiled. 'Shouldn't we all think like that?' he said.

Amy's mother looked perplexed, and then dismissive; muttering just above her breath—about calling Zoë, and putting the trifle back in the fridge—she began to slide away from the rest of the group. Grandma and Grandad followed her, shuffling along like bags on a conveyor belt.

Michael was still smiling wanly, and when Amy looked around she saw that her father was nodding back at him, his face alight with admiration. He nodded again as he stood aside, gesturing to Michael to go before him, bowing his head a little as Michael passed.

'We should all think like that,' he said quietly in agreement, and he continued to nod as he followed Michael down the hallway, matching his steps, the two of them turning—a small procession—into the faded evening light of the living room.

Going Under

Tim and Bella were on their way to the lake, on a balmy April evening, when they hit something on the road, something bigger than a possum or rabbit, something that made a *thud* against the front of the car, an almost human sound.

Bella cried out, as if it was her, hurt on the road. She covered her eyes like a child.

It was just after six, and the sunlight was bending down over the hills, in through the windscreen. Bella had been dozing, her head rolling back and forth across the headrest, her mouth slightly open, showing the edge of her pink tongue. Tim looked at her, just for a second, and suddenly wondered what he was doing, in this car, with this woman. He had wondered that, and felt a slight stirring at the top of his stomach, a fluttery uneasiness, and then *thud,* they had hit it, and Bella's eyes were open, wide.

They had set out just after three.

It was a plan they had had, ever since meeting, to take off for a weekend, just hop in the car and drive and see where they ended up. The thought of it was exhilarating, as if planned spontaneity could actually seem spontaneous once the plan was in action.

'Wouldn't that be fun?' Bella said to him, tugging the end of his finger, using a tone that sounded like she wasn't sure if it would or wouldn't be and needed reassurance. She pursed her lips a little, waiting for his response. 'Don't you think? Fun?'

Tim said, Yes, yes it would. He sounded like he meant it. He did.

Bella had been given Friday off work and her call wasn't until 11.00 on Monday. She had a main part in an English TV series shooting in the studios on the edge of town. Cast and crew came cheap in these parts, Bella said. It was like shipping in black slaves—or going to the slaves, actually. And yet it wasn't slavery, it was a hell of a good gig to get—well paid, fun. She played a medieval warrior princess with some ridiculous name, which was hard to imagine, given her short dark hair and diminutive size. She wore a wig, apparently made of human hair, all the way from Russia, and silicone pouches stuffed in her bra.

Smoke and mirrors, Bella had said to Tim hazily, and he felt suitably impressed, although the statement seemed intended for him not to be. It was as if he had his finger on the pulse, as if he were in the presence of a magician's apprentice, or a magician even, keeping her cloak under wraps just for now.

Tim had picked Bella up from her flat, and had felt exhilarated for a moment, just as he'd hoped he would. She reminded him of a Jack Russell, some sort of small, strong little dog, nicely compact, perfectly packaged. She had a quick, definite quality about her movement, as if she was always in a hurry, always on important business.

'Hi-de-hi,' she called to him as he drew up in the car. She was standing on the pavement with her bags by her feet. She swivelled herself from side to side. 'Howdy cowboy,' she said. 'Howdy.'

Tim smiled at her and tweaked her waist with his fingertips.

'Hi there,' he said, and winked. A soft pulsing moved through his chest, like the time he touched Patricia Clarke's thigh in the movies when they were fifteen. Patricia was his best friend's girlfriend and wasn't his to touch. The feeling had started at his toes and moved up towards his neck, almost choking him. Every now and then he got that with Bella: that forbidden surge. He was fourteen years her senior—nearly old enough to be her father—and he felt it sometimes when she looked at him with her bright, impish eyes and said things like that: things like howdy, and cowboy, in her light youthful way, as if life was really a bit of a joke.

But he liked it today, the way she said it. He liked the feeling it gave him. He was on the verge of an adventure, albeit a dangerous one.

'Fun!' Bella said. 'What fun.' And she slid into the passenger seat.

They headed north. It was warm and still, and at first they drove with the windows down, feeling the air move around the car, in under their clothes. Once they were on the main road Bella seemed unusually weary, subdued. She looked out the open window and blinked fast, presumably to try to counter the wind in her eyes. She yawned even, a couple of times, and ran her hand up and down her neck. Tim wondered if she was bored, if he should be entertaining her. He turned on the radio, and just about drove into a ditch, looking for a station. Bella didn't seem to notice. She smiled at him vaguely when he looked at her. She placed one hand in her lap.

They stopped in some small town with an unpronounce-able name for a coffee at the local tearooms. Bella was charmed, she said, by the Formica tables and netting curtains, and the rotund woman who served them who wore an apron that looked like a doily round her waist.

'It's so cute, isn't it?' she said. 'Quaint.' She leaned over the table towards him as she said it, and a fleck of spit shot out her mouth and landed somewhere—Tim couldn't see where. For the first time that day, for the first time since he had met her, in fact, he felt a pang of disapproval, even embarrassment for her.

'It smells like dirty hair, to me,' he said. 'Places like this are the places of my childhood. Quaint isn't the word. Depressing, I would say.'

Bella looked at him quite blankly, as if she hadn't heard what he said. She blinked rapidly, just as she'd been doing in the car—it clearly wasn't the wind—and then she made a sound in her throat, a soft sort of *humph*. She slid out of her chair and sauntered up to the counter to get herself some gum.

They got on the road again, still with no clear destination in mind, but they were heading in the direction of the lake—that's where the road was taking them. Bella found a tape in the glove box, slipped it on, and rested her head against the headrest and chewed away at her gum. The sun was getting lower, and the paddocks and trees were bathed in it. They slipped by, field after field, fence after fence, and then the road grew steeper, started to climb upwards, winding a little as it did so.

Bella rested her hand on the back of Tim's neck, fiddling her fingers through his hair. Her skin felt cool, he thought, like water. She spoke every now and then, pausing in her chewing to remark on something out the window, something that always seemed to have passed by the time Tim turned his head to look. He continued to try, though, feeling somehow that he was missing out on all the fun. It seemed to make Bella edgy, his rubbernecking, even though it was she who was instigating it.

'Never mind,' she said to him after a while, almost tersely. 'Let's not drive off the road!' And then she flicked the gum out of its resting place in her cheek, and started chewing again, not loudly, but with a certain vigour, an elasticity.

They climbed higher and higher, and Bella started to blink slowly. Tim could see that out of the corner of his eyes. She closed her lids intermittently, lifted them, closed them, and then, suddenly, she seemed to be asleep. Her head lolled a little and her mouth was open, and Tim wondered if he should hook a finger inside her cheek to rescue the gum, to stop her from choking. He wanted to do it, wanted to search around in there against her tongue, almost wanted her to open her eyes while he was doing it, get a fright. But he didn't. He just kept a watch on her carefully, noticing the white downy hair on her neck— illuminated by the sun—and the line of three tiny moles dotted along her hairline, and then he felt that sense, the sudden uneasiness, and then they hit it, and Bella opened her eyes and cried out, seemingly in pain.

It was a bird.

That's what they'd hit. And Bella wouldn't get out of the car. She kept her fingers over her eyes, and made a low sound in her throat like the far-off drone of an engine.

The car was stopped in the middle of the road, and Tim stood there, with his arms crossed over his chest, and he felt shaky, shakier than he would have expected to. It was not just a bird, it was a hawk. And it wasn't dead.

Bella's voice came snaking out through the open door.

'Okay,' she said. 'What is it? Tim? Is it very bad?' She paused. 'Tim?'

He swallowed hard.

The hawk was half sitting, half lying on the road, one wing outstretched awkwardly. The other was tucked in under itself, and its neck bent down towards that side, as if it could tuck its head under there too. Tim could see one open eye, and its beak, which was opening and shutting on itself, opening and shutting like a mechanical gate that was broken, stuck in one repetitive movement. There was a streak of blood on the road—not much, but enough—and it was coming out in one thin line from somewhere under its body.

'Tim?' Bella called. 'Is it bad?'

He took one step, tentatively, towards it. The hawk tried to move itself, dragging its outstretched wing a couple of centimetres along the road, but then it fell back onto its side, breathing heavily. The lower side of its body seemed to be crushed, one leg hardly there at all.

'Christ,' Tim said. 'Would you come and help me please, Bella?'

She didn't respond.

'Now?'

'What *is* it?' she cried.

*

They had met a month before at a friend's birthday dinner at some swanky restaurant in town.

Tim hadn't even noticed Bella for the first half of the evening. She was at the other end of the table, and didn't seem especially worth noticing. That's how it seemed to him at the time. But somehow, as the night wore on, they ended up sitting next to each other, and she turned to him as if he were a pet project.

'So,' she said. 'Tell me. Are you having fun?' She whispered the last part, conspiratorially. He could smell her breath against his cheek, the twang on it from the wine. Her nose twitched slightly. She was cute.

Tim suddenly felt happy, a great rush of it. He laughed.

'I am, as a matter of fact,' he said. 'I am now.'

Later, she leaned over as if to whisper something in his ear, and licked the lobe instead: a quick flick of her tongue, like a cat.

Much later, she slid her warm little hand under his shirt at the back and rested it there above his belt, against the skin.

How could he refuse?

*

The hawk was in the back seat, loosely wrapped in a sweatshirt. Its bad wing sprouted out from under the fabric, so big that it made Tim's chest do a little thump every time he looked at it. Every now and then the sweatshirt shifted. It was Bella's, and had 'Hawaii' printed on its front. She didn't even like it, she said. She was glad for it to be put to good use. She didn't seem to be able to put herself to good use though. Every time she looked at the hawk she cried out, though the cries were getting fainter and fainter as time went along. She couldn't touch it, she said. She was sorry, but she just couldn't.

The sun had gone down, and they drove in silence. It was not totally dark yet, just a heavy tainted grey, and the headlights swung across the road in front of them as they wound down the hill.

'Where did it come from?' Tim said. 'I didn't even see it. How could that be?'

Bella was driving, and she flicked one hand up off the steering wheel. She touched his hand, lightly, and he noticed how much hotter it was now, slightly wet.

'Let's talk about something else,' she said. 'Hey? Let's just change the subject.'

The sweatshirt rippled.

Tim rubbed at his face. 'I'm pretty tired, Bella,' he said. 'I don't really feel like playing let's pretend.'

It sounded sharper than he'd meant it to. He heard her exhale slightly, a little puff coming out from between her closed lips. She lifted her hand up off his and returned it to the steering wheel.

'Sorry,' he said.

'No, I'm sorry,' she said. 'I'm sorry not to be much help. I'm sorry our weekend is ruined. I'm sorry you hit the damn thing.' She made a little clicking sound in her throat, licked her lips. She turned the tape back on, and the music lurched into the car, cutting in right in the middle of a song.

They came across the Oasis Motel just after eight. It had a large lit-up sign with two palm trees on it, a bright blue pool of water, a hibiscus flower. The top left-hand corner of the sign had been smashed so that the edge of the flower was gone, the yellow cylinder of light pulsing behind it. It was like seeing under a woman's skirt, Tim thought, and discovering that she was wearing beige underpants. Maybe not as bad as that, actually, but still. He ran his hands through his hair.

The motel seemed to be in the middle of nowhere. Its white sign had blinked at them even when they were miles away from it, even before they could make out what it was. It had seemed like a haze of bland light hovering somewhere above the land, just at the edge of the horizon. As they got closer they could make out the palm trees, the unnatural-looking pool of water beneath them, the flower, its jagged edge. There were rows of separate units, all with lights on, dotted along the mini porches. The main building was lit up like a Christmas tree. Yellow light bled out of every window, out into the night. It was impossible to tell where they were, if they were close or far away from the lake. But it was dark now, and Tim didn't really care any more.

Bella swerved into the entrance and turned off the engine, and then the headlights, with a small flick of her wrist. They sat in the dark, side by side, with the feeling of the hawk behind them, though no sound was coming from the back seat now at all.

'They might know of an afterhours vet,' Tim said. 'I'm sure they'll know what the best thing is to do.'

'Yeah, sure,' Bella said. 'An afterhours vet, right in the middle of the wops. That's right, city boy.' She laughed bitterly, and then patted his hand. 'Sorry,' she said. 'But, you know.'
She leaned towards him then, straining against the belt, and kissed the edge of his face. Her lips felt too warm, and moist, like her hand.

'I'm sorry,' she said again. 'I just can't stand this. This whole thing.'

He could feel the small puffs of air coming out her nose, yet she stayed there with her face pressed against his, almost as if she had fallen asleep. He touched her bare knee with his fingertips, lowered his whole hand cautiously onto the skin. She shifted herself, slightly, towards him.

'Fighting already,' she whispered. 'It's a bad sign.'

Tim pecked the edge of her nose, and her cheek, and up a bit, right at the corner of her eye.

'Yes,' he said. 'But it'll be okay. Promise.'

He got out of the car.

*

Tim had met his wife, Jennifer, when they were both eighteen. They had married six months later, and had stayed like that—married, that is—for eighteen years. Eighteen + eighteen, Tim often thought, equals disaster. Not that it was—not a disaster exactly, more of a puttering out, as if they started with too much of a bang, too steady a belief in the power of their supposed love, and then just ran out of gas one day in the middle of nowhere.

Jen had gone in all the wrong directions, she said. Career, no kids. She wanted to start anew. She moved to Australia, and remarried within a year, a car salesman, BMWs or something. She had a baby now, had sent Tim a photo at Christmas, with a card that was friendly but distant. The kid looked nothing like her: it was fair, with a smudge of white hair on the top of its head, and small, fat hands. Tim had looked at the photo for hours, not because he liked babies especially, but because the baby was sitting on her lap. He recognised her hands, the tan of her skin, the veins pressing up underneath it, curling up under her sleeve. He could see her hair too, just the ends of it, slightly brittle, thick. Love Jen, she had scrawled on the back. Love Jen—like a plea, instead of a signing off.

That's how it seemed to him at the time, anyway: as if there was a message there, in those two words, the meaning seemingly changed just because there was no comma between them. Love Jen—scrawled, smudged, an afterthought perhaps, an attempt at softening the blow of sending a card and picture advertising her new life. It was nothing more than that, of course, and he didn't even want it to be. That was just the feeling he got when he read the words. Love Jen. *Please.*

That was at Christmas, and now it was April. He'd been seeing Mandy Smart then, just casually, but that hadn't even lasted into the New Year.

And now he was seeing Bella. An *actress.* He could put that in a card to Jen. Here's a photo of my new partner, it could say, who is an actress in an extremely popular TV series. This is her in costume, it could say. Love Tim.

*

The door of the reception had an old-fashioned bell on it, and it tinkled nervously as he stepped inside.

The walls were panelled in a pale wood, had framed pictures hanging on them, fishing memorabilia, as far as Tim could tell. Even though, from the outside, the lights had seemed glaringly bright, inside everything was dim. It was as if the air was filled with smoke, a dusty soft smoke, almost a fog. The air smelt faintly—Tim couldn't tell what of, perfume, soap, an attempt at masking tobacco probably. He stood by the counter and waited. The bell at the door hadn't brought any staff running from the barracks. He pressed the button on the counter-top, not holding it down too long, not wanting to seem impatient. He heard footsteps on the floor above him then, though they were more like the sound of a dead body being heaved around up there.

Tim craned his neck to try and read the papers strewn across the reception desk, ran his foot back and forth across the carpet. A car door slammed outside. The front door opened, setting the bell off, letting out a shimmer of sound. Tim turned, expecting Bella, but it wasn't her at all, and the woman who moved into the reception shot right past him, lifting up the counter-top, ducking under, landing in the seat behind the desk like a large bird on the surface of a pond. Her flesh, mostly concealed under a floral kaftan, seemed to shudder for a moment, almost in her wake, though of course it wasn't, just all around her, soft and voluminous, moist-looking.

'Stairs broke,' she said to Tim abruptly, her small eyes blinking hard.

He didn't know what she meant.

'Sorry?'

'Stairs broke,' she said again, in exactly the same tone, 'so I have to come down the outside. Every time. I've called the builder three times. Could've broke my damn neck. Or worse.' She smiled then, as if it was funny, though she clearly didn't think it was. 'Sorry to keep you waiting,' she said, and smiled again, added, 'Sir,' like a child who had just remembered its manners.

Tim tried to smile back. He felt overwhelmed by tiredness.

'We're after a double room,' he said, 'a double room, and a recommendation for where we could find some dinner, and we have a little problem—' he paused— 'that I'm hoping you may be able to help me with.'

The woman still had her lips pinched upwards, though

Tim realised it was more of a default setting than a smile. Her face was just set that way.

'Try me,' she said.

Tim swallowed.

'I have a bird in the car,' he said, 'a sick—well, a hurt bird, really. I hit it, you see. On the road. It's a hawk.' He stopped, scratched at his neck.

The woman narrowed her eyes at him as if she'd just stepped out into a great wind.

'A hawk,' she said.

'Yes.'

'That you hit on the road.'

'Regrettably, yes.'

'Mr . . . ?'

'Sheridan.'

'Mr Sheridan.' She shuffled her hands round the computer. The skin of her forearms swayed as she did so, slowly, back and forth. 'Mr Sheridan, we have a no pets policy in our rooms.'

She slapped a laminated sign down triumphantly on the counter. No Pets, it said. Et cetera, et cetera.

'We have a no pets policy,' she said again. She smiled.

'It isn't a pet,' Tim said quietly, 'and we don't want it sleeping in our bed, I can assure you. It's half dead. There must be someone we can call for help.' He waved his arms around, feeling stranded. 'There must be someone we can call,' he said, raising his voice ever so slightly, 'who'll know what to do.'

The woman opened and shut her mouth several times. Her hair was dyed cherry red, had grey roots that looked more out of place, somehow, than the lurid brassiness beyond them. It was cut short and had the fluffy shapelessness of brushed cotton.

'Oh, I don't think so,' she said. There was laughter lurking somewhere in behind her voice. 'Help you? With a half-dead hawk?' Her lips curled up—default setting. 'No, Mr Sheridan,' she said. 'I don't think so.'

'No vet you know of who I could call? No?'

She did a little shake of her head, and made a sound in her throat to accompany it.

'No ideas at all?'

Another shake.

Tim started to back towards the door.

'Never mind,' he said. 'Forget it. Forget the room. I'll sort it out. Thanks anyway.'

She leaned back in her chair. 'What I would've said—' she cocked her chin at him, lifted one dappled arm up towards the counter— 'what I would've said is, don't pick it up in the first place. That's what I would've told you. Leave it, I would've said. That's my advice.'

'I wish you'd been there to give it to me then,' Tim said. 'It would have been helpful, I'm sure.'

'Sherry's being killed off upstairs,' she said. She glanced at the clock on the wall, and Tim was suddenly aware of its ticking, slightly irregular. 'I've almost missed it,' she said. 'Sherry's last show.'

Tim was by the door, and he reached for the handle.

'I interrupted you. Sorry.'

'My advice,' she called after him, 'would be to put it back on the road, let someone finish off what you started. Sad, Mr Sheridan, but true!'

He let the door clang back into place behind him.

Bella was sitting on the bonnet of the car. She had her legs folded up against her body, her arms holding her knees. He couldn't see the expression on her face; it looked smooth, featureless.

'How'd it go?' she said.

Behind him, Tim heard the door of the reception open and then shut again. The woman started down the ramp, wobbling a little. She was wearing her slippers—he hadn't noticed that before. They flapped against her feet, making a soft squelching sound. She kept her head down, as if she didn't know they were there.

'Not so good,' he said. He almost laughed.

*

In the last year of their marriage, Jen's cat had died. It was old, and its death was well overdue, but it still felt like an omen, a metaphor for their already failed relationship. It was twenty-one, a silver-haired Persian, and its fur had taken on the qualities of a soiled rug in a skip. It had lost clumps of flesh to cancer, maybe even an organ or two. Nearing the end, it could hardly even meow. Tim referred to it as The Doorstop.

Still, Jen was devastated. And Tim, despite himself, was somewhat stricken too. They brought it home from the vet, wrapped in a pink baby blanket, its body strangely heavy, feeling more full, more solid, than when they'd carried it in alive.

Tim dug a hole in the back yard, and they put it in and covered it over with dirt. Afterwards Jen lay down, placed the side of her face against the earthy mound like a doctor listening to a child's chest. He should have lain down there with her—wanted to, even—but he didn't, just went inside to put tea on. He could see the dark shape of her body from the kitchen window, the stillness of it. After half an hour, maybe more, she raised herself up slowly, just like something coming back from the dead. He could hear the softness of her feet padding down the hallway, the sound of the shower being turned on.

She came into the kitchen wearing only her underpants and one sock.

'Help me, please,' she said, and for a moment he thought she was asking him to take it away, the pain; to hold her or something. But she only meant with her necklace, the clasp. He fumbled with it against her neck.

There were two spindly twigs, caught there, in her hair.

*

They started driving again, the hum of the Oasis Motel getting smaller and smaller behind them until it was swallowed suddenly by the black. It seemed as if they were driving backwards, as if leaving the light behind was wrong somehow, as if they should be crawling towards it instead. They had not eaten for hours, but neither of them mentioned it, and perhaps neither of them needed to. Tim didn't feel hungry certainly.

The hawk still shifted from time to time in the back seat—a soft feathery scraping. Bella no longer cried out when she heard it, but lifted her hand to her face as if to muffle the sound that wasn't coming out anyway. She seemed so small to Tim, sitting there in the seat beside him. He could hardly relate her to the woman who had flicked her tongue against his skin in the restaurant the night they met; the brashness of her hand sliding under his shirt in a room full of people; her unbuckling his belt in the car. She seemed so cool to him then, putting the show on the road, running it. And now, perched in the passenger seat, with the bleeding bird and a bad afternoon behind her, she seemed like the opposite, yes, the opposite, of everything he'd thought she was.

'How old are your parents?' she said to him, quite out of the blue, as if it was something she had wanted to know all along and had only just found the words.

'Seventies. Yours?'

'Their fifties.'

She was almost smiling, her face turned slightly towards him and the road also. Something in her expression made him tap down lightly on the accelerator, as if a little more speed was the answer, though he didn't know what the question was.

It had begun to rain, just a drizzle really, a wet mist frosting the windscreen. The wipers squeaked against the glass.

'You'll have to kill it, Tim,' she said. 'You know that, don't you.'

'Yes,' he said. 'I do.'

And then the silence descended on them again, like a faint smell.

—

It seemed, in a way, that the lake found them.

The road, the hills and trees all around, the white markers, the headlights rolling on in front—it had all felt endless. And then suddenly there was the water, smooth and dark, the land opening out to accommodate it. A sound came out Bella's mouth, but it wasn't anguish, it was a sing-song sort of sigh; it was relief.

Tim swerved onto the gravel and turned off the engine.

It was half-past nine.

They opened the windows, and the drizzle angled in, tapping against their faces.

'You have to kill it,' Bella said again. She stared straight ahead.

Tim sat dead still, his hands pressed against his knees. From somewhere under the bonnet of the car came a ticking sound, loud and irregular. His breath seemed to match it—or that's how it seemed to him—but Bella's beside him was steady and slow, hardly audible. He waited for her to say something else but she didn't. She wound the window down a little, and then up a little, and continued looking out through the windscreen.

'How about if I said *you* had to kill it,' he said. 'Then what would you do?'

It was a question he didn't want an answer to particularly, and a question he knew it wasn't really fair to ask. He could, if he wanted, fool himself into believing he was truly interested in the answer. But it wasn't that. It was her *response* that interested him.

Bella paused, and drew her tongue across her top lip.

'I'd probably get out and walk home,' she said, and then

she turned her face square towards him and smiled an odd little smile, its edges slightly jagged. 'Why, Tim?' she said, smiling all the time. '*Are* you going to ask me that?' The whites of her eyes were lit up by the lights on the dashboard and the headlights outside.

She shook her head. '*Are* you?' she said again.

There seemed to be a hardening in the skin round her jaw. Something in the way she held her teeth—tight together, the bottoms bared—made the skin all round her mouth and under her cheeks look like it had set.

Tim tried to laugh, though the sound that came out of his mouth was more like a warble.

'No of course not,' he said. 'I'm sorry. Ignore me. I was just trying to make a joke.'

He smiled at her in the hope she would smile back, but she had already turned her face towards the windscreen again, and she was looking out it, peering even, as though she was waiting for something—anything—to appear in front of her on the road.

'Well, ha-ha,' she said.

Tim got out of the car, opened the back door, leaned in across the passenger seat. The hawk was hard to grasp, covered in the sweatshirt, its broken wing falling right to the floor. He felt its resistance, though it didn't struggle, and for a moment he hoped that it was just the resistance of bone, and that it may already be dead. It was wishful thinking, for sure. As he tried to angle the wing out the door, it wavered slightly, and then rose sharply towards his face. It just about hit him in the eye. It seemed to take all his strength to get it contained again, pressed tight against his chest. He tried not to pay attention to the fact that the fabric—Bella's Hawaii sweatshirt—felt wet under his hands: wet and sticky, but cold.

Tim moved down the bank and across the pebbles and onto the sand. The sound of the lake, slapping in and out, was loud, so close-sounding, it could have been right upon him. He turned back towards the car. Bella had turned the internal light on, and the doors were open, and she sat in the whiteness, staring straight ahead, quite still. Her head looked small and dark, like the top of a pin, and he suddenly felt that his whole life was in that car, though of course it wasn't. That was the only life he had right at that moment, though: her, and the hawk, and the water, and the heavy throb of the sky above them, releasing gusts of wet into the air.

Go to her, something said to him, inside.

He laid the hawk down on the sand and moved his body down beside it. He was muttering to himself, trying to stay calm. When he peeled the sweatshirt back the hawk lifted slightly, out towards the air. In the dark he could hardly see, and he was glad of that, glad to be spared the mess he had made. The hawk seemed more alive than it should, he thought, considering everything it had lost. It clawed at the air with its one leg, its beak opening and shutting, creaking softly. As Tim lifted its body out of the sweatshirt, he felt where the fabric stuck a little to a wound, the soft tear as he pulled the two apart.

Up close its feathers smelt slightly sweet, like freshly dug earth. There was a strange smoothness to them, the rise of bones somewhere deep under all that downiness, under the flesh. Its chest was against his, and far off he could feel a pounding, though it could have just been him, his own heart. It beat its wing against his shoulder. He moved his hands to hold it tighter, and as he did his fingers sank into a patch where the feathers were gone, sliding right inside, touching something that felt like bone. It felt so hot in there, as if it should be steaming. Tim cried out and stumbled, and felt something cool move up around his feet, into his shoes, sucking up his trouser legs.

It was the lake.

The suddenness of its being upon him made his knees give way. He felt his body fold down into the water like someone into prayer. The bird fell soundlessly out of his arms, sliding across his stomach, into the lake. It was still for a moment, seemingly resting on the surface, and then the water started to draw it down. It pounded its wing against Tim's torso, arching its body towards him, its neck curling in the dark; a sound came out its beak that was hardly a sound at all, more like a far-off squealing, so faint and desperate it seemed to Tim it was simply inside his own head. He pressed his hands against its feathers, pushed its body firmly under, pushed until he felt it grate the bottom. The water was up to his elbows, and up to his stomach, and all round his legs, a part of his shoes. There was a soft heaving against his palms, faint as a pulse. The water quaked.

Tim turned his head away, scanning for the car.

Bella hadn't moved, the soft fog of drizzle surrounding her, and it looked to him as if she was floating up there in that ball of light, like a plastic figure in a toy plane.

Go to her, the voice said again, but he turned his head away, shaking it slightly; turned to look out across the lake.

Far off, on the other shore, he could see lights, a whole gaggle of them, a powdery yellow in the mist. They seemed to be blinking, winking even. And he blinked back, the fever in his throat beginning to slide down, out of reach, back into the water. There were lights on either side of him—Bella in the car, the town in the distance; him in the dark, surrounded, holding the hawk's body down. He would stay there a little longer, he thought, right there inside the lake, the water moving round the edges of him, where it met the air. And when he was ready he would let it go, that mound of wet feathers beneath his hands. He would lift himself out of the lake. He would watch as the hawk's body came rising up through the soft water to meet him.

The Beekeeper

A True Story

When she was seventeen, my mother saved her own life just by walking across the lawn to the washing line.

It was summer. She was woken that morning by the heat, she says—and by the phone, ringing downstairs. She was home for her university holidays. When she picked up the receiver there was a voice on the line that she'd never heard before. A young man's voice—shaky—asking her to meet him outside the movie theatre on Main Street. Who's this? she said to him. Who's this? He refused to say. My mother, light-heartedly, laughing it off, said, No.

It was an ordinary weekday morning, perhaps a

Tuesday, and the whole family—except for my mother—had gone away. They lived in Stark Street, up on the hill, in an old house overlooking the town, and the river, and the bare hills rolling towards the sky. My mother tells me that you could see mountains to the north and the west from the windows in the upstairs bedrooms. But when I try to picture those bedrooms, and the windows, and the mountains, I can't. All I can see is the verandahs all the way round, upstairs and down, and the plants hanging in crocheted baskets from the ceiling, and the staircase, long and dark and curving. My grandfather chasing me up it on his hands and knees. Pretending to be a bear.

There is a lawn too. It is a bright soft green and it is wide and slightly curved, dipping down over the hill. There is a dirt path leading down the side of a bank in steep loops, and a tangle of nasturtiums. And then nothing. Nothing in my head, that is. Strange how memory works, how you can be so *in* something you can almost taste it, and then one step further and bang! You're over a cliff with your eyes closed. Nothing.

I can see that lawn, though. It's big and wide, stretching out in every direction. My mother is on that lawn. She is young, wild-eyed, and moving across it so rapidly in her smooth bare feet. She is running faster than she's ever run before; her heart, pumping in time with her feet; her feet, pounding the earth.

My mother is in the house, in an upstairs bedroom, when she hears the front door open and then shut again. It is nearly 10 a.m. She has just showered and her hair is dripping down her back and down her front, a wet clump of it heavy against her neck. Hello? she calls into the morning. Hello-o? There is no answer. She walks out of her room and down the hall and begins to move, slowly, down the staircase. Her hand on the banister. Hello?

Perhaps she senses him there before she gets to the bottom, before she turns into the dimness of the hallway. That's why she's moving slowly, I guess. Cautiously. Feeling each step with her feet. Who's there? she says. Who's there?

He is. The man from the phone. She is sure of that as soon as she sees him there.

He's standing stock still near the end of the hallway, and he doesn't say, Me, or, I am, or, Hello back. He just stands there, looking foolish, a bandana tied over his face, just his eyes showing, his damp forehead, and a black-handled knife in his hand.

My mother comes to an abrupt halt. They stand facing each other, perhaps a metre apart. His hand with the knife moves, just a touch, but everything else is still.

Her whole body seems to fill with air, a great rush of it. She could float away right there; she is that light. She tries to smile without showing any sign of alarm, to smile without showing her teeth.

Don't be silly, she says fluidly. Do you want a cup of tea?

*

My grandparents were great fans of bottling. They had wallpapered the rooms of the house in large seventies prints, and the front garden was filled with fruit trees. An enormous flowering plum drooped over the front gate and dripped plums and juice all over the footpath. There were more plums than anyone could eat. My grandparents grew resourceful. They filled buckets with fruit from the garden and made their own wine—thick liquors that looked like sugar syrup. They did this for a decade, maybe two, storing the wine, and dusty jars of bottled peaches and plums, apricots and nectarines, in a large cupboard in that downstairs hallway.

My mother thought, briefly, about trying to hide in there. She stood in the hallway with her arms crossed over her chest, trying to hide the shape of her skin under the light fabric. Wanting to hide her whole self. Get in the cupboard.

No, too late now.

The cupboard, or the back door, or the living-room window. Surely she could get out of there; she had opened it that very morning.

It's just like people say, apparently. You're half in, and you're half out. You sort of slow down and speed up at the same time. You're just raw animal, absorbing each second. Every thought, she says, was like a drop of water falling into a glass. Tink, tink. Crystal clear and achingly steady. No wild rambling in there. Just a thought. Tink. And then another. Tink.

*

The man with the knife is waving his arm around, almost in slow motion, like it's a flag and he's surrendering. Her whole body is pumping blood; her heart is working double time. She is filled up with her own life. Do not show the whites of your eyes, she tells herself. Do not show you are afraid. She offers him that cup of tea, calmly, kindly, keeping it light, and he says, no. Of course. No, that's not what he wants at all.

From somewhere outside she hears a sound, far off, the groan of machinery, perhaps a lawn mower. The sound could come closer, she thinks. Could it come through the gate and up the path and into the hallway, flashing its loud blades? She listens hard, but it dies away. Clack clack clack.

She can smell sweat when the man moves his arms about, which he's beginning to do more frantically. Jolting around like fish caught on a line. He's starting to pant, and his breathing seems to propel him forward, his feet stepping across the carpet towards her. She can tell that he's not much older than her—maybe nineteen, twenty at the most. He holds the knife out in front of him. He'll use it, he says. The knife. If she doesn't do exactly what he tells her to. She nods. Yes, yes, she says, I understand.

He leads her into the living room.

Let's just sit down for a minute, she says. Okay? Let's just sit down.

They do. Side by side on the couch. She tries not to look at him, but she catches a flash of his forehead, which is dripping wet, and an awful scaly red round its edges. The smell of his skin, and of his tucked-in beige shirt, is right beside her now. His cuffs are tightly buttoned, done up tight around his wrists, like bandages. A breeze is coming in the open window, but he's right there with the knife, holding it stiffly in his hand, and it's clear she's not going anywhere without him. The sun is innocently filling the room with light. A thought comes into her head—tink—and then slides out again. Tink.

I know you, I know you—this is what he says to her, over and over again. I know you.

But she has never seen him before in her life. It's hard to tell, I guess, with the bandana over his face, but she can feel that she doesn't know him. His rough blond hair. His panting voice. They're ringing no bells. No bells here.

He moves closer to her and starts clawing at her nightie. He's pulling so hard on it that it feels like it will just rip right open, right there. She tries to take his hand in hers and hold it still, but he's stronger than her, of course, and he breaks away, back onto the fabric, back onto her skin.

My mother realises that maybe there's nothing she can do. This realisation comes to her almost quietly; it is as if she hears it from a distance. It does not come with the sort of weight she might have expected. I can't get away, she thinks to herself, and she hears only the words, not what they mean. She is sweating too, her hands hot and prickly, drips sliding down from under her arms. Her hair feels slimy against her neck. She looks at a picture on the opposite wall. She looks at the wallpaper with its coloured squares. She talks, all the while, like her mother might to her younger siblings, who are all still little, school aged, somewhere in a car, somewhere with her parents. She talks in a voice, and with a tone, in a way she has never talked before.

Everything's okay, she says to the man with the knife. Let's just sit here a little longer.

But he says, No. No, no, *no!* And he starts saying these terrible things to her, how he wants to hurt her, and how he's going to have her, whether she likes it or not. He sort of laughs as he says it, but he is shaking a lot, she sees, his hands and his knife, sweat sliding down his face onto the fabric of his bandana. His voice is shaking too.

My mother makes a sudden decision. She needs to get outside. She knows she can't escape from him, but if she can get outside it will all be okay. This is what she tells herself. Get out.

She slows her voice right down and she says to the man, I need to get the washing in.

This is the best she can think of. It has been out for an hour and a half at most. It will still be dripping. She doesn't care.

I need to get the washing in, she says. Calmly, persistently. You can do whatever you want to me, but first I need to get the washing in.

He's getting confused. It's not going to plan. She can tell this. He has not rehearsed for this scene. He waves his knife around.

You'll scream, he says.

No I won't, she says. How can I? You've got a knife.

One of his feet is tapping against the carpet. He looks as if he might wriggle out of his own skin. You'll scream, he says again.

No I won't, my mother repeats, in exactly the same tone. I promise you, she says.

He goes still. His neck becomes quite limp, drooping

towards his chest. She realises it's a nod, or a half nod, slow and pronounced. He mumbles a reply. Something like, Hurry then, be quick.

He stands up before her and they walk out through the french doors together, like a couple heading out to enjoy the sun, the fresh morning air. If someone had been over on the opposite hill, watching, they would have thought them quite happy, quite calm, my mother and this man, moving down across the deck, onto the grass, his hand close to her back.

*

When I was small I loved bees. I would carry them round in my hands. What's that? my mother used to say—what's that you've got in there?—before prising my fingers open to reveal pulsing wings, a sharply pointed little back. I made coffins out of matchboxes—coffins filled with cotton wool—when I found their little curled bodies closed in on themselves, and dried up, on the footpath. I had a stack of them, these cardboard tombs, in my room.

My mother's feet—pale and smooth, moving across the grass—must have called to them that day. To the bees. They must have. Because a bee came and slipped its body under her. Arching its back up towards her skin.

She feels the sting dart right up through her foot, into her leg. The flailing, bumbling wings on the grass. She cries out, and the man with the knife grabs her lips with his fingers to silence her. But she *has* been stung, he can see that; her foot begins to swell, redder and fatter every second. She starts to cry.

I'm allergic, she sobs. You have to help me, I'm allergic.

The man with the knife shifts from foot to foot, and wipes the sweat off his brow, and breathes fast and high, like a panting dog.

My mother's thoughts are rapid now. It is as if a window has opened in the world for her to slip through.

You must get me some vinegar, she cries. From the kitchen. The pantry. Please, I'm allergic. Please.

You'll run away, he says. No! You'll run away!

But down on the grass, cradling her fat shiny foot, she cries even harder.

How can I? she says. I can't even walk. You must help me!

He takes a few steps, then turns to look at her, and takes a few more and turns again. The knife dangles in his hand. He strides, half runs, across the length of the grass, up onto the deck. Inside.

She is off the ground and onto her feet in one liquid movement. She runs towards the fence, feet hardly touching the ground she's moving so fast. Over a fence.

Bang! Bang! on the neighbour's door. Nobody home. Over another fence. Bang! bang! Nobody home. And another. And one more.

The fourth house my mother went to that morning was not empty.

She banged on the door with the sides of her fists and

her elbows and her knees. She could see a figure coming down the hallway, moving slowly, blurry in the yellow tempered glass. The door opened, and she slipped through it, back into her life.

*

There are no photos of my mother from around this time. There are the school ones, of course—row upon row of straight-backed girls, uniforms on, expressionless. And there are two creased black and white shots showing her and a group of friends fooling around on the school field. She has long plaits that have been caught mid-sway, curving upwards in the air. She is laughing, her mouth wide open.

And then there is a gap of years. In the next photo she must be twenty-one, maybe even twenty-two. It is in colour, but faded, so that everything, even the blue of her high-waisted flared jeans, has a slightly sepia tone. Her rust-red hair looks as if it's been mixed with milk. She and a friend stand on a concrete step, the weatherboard of the house behind them only faintly there. Neither of them is smiling at all.

*

The carpet is a dusky floral in the house my mother bursts into. She slams the door shut behind her, and the carpet rises up, its bouquets apricot-coloured, sage green. Really it is just her legs giving way, the sudden swoop of the flowers coming to meet her. The man who has opened the door wears a white suit from head to toe, and smells faintly of smoke. He stands over her, his face weary-looking with astonishment, listening to the sounds her tongue is making, the words not coming out straight, not even in the right order. The light in there is dim—not just in the hallway, but in the living room, which he leads her into, calling for his wife.

We were outside, he says to my mother. In the garden. When I heard you knocking. I was doing the bees.

He is wearing gloves, she notices then, and carries a netting hat in one hand.

His wife appears, and stops in the doorway when she sees her, this girl in a transparent nightie, her whole body shuddering on the couch. The woman has curlers in her hair, but she must think to herself that it doesn't matter now—she must think this when she sees my mother, her breasts showing through.

They move around the house, then, this man and his wife. The locks on the doors going click click click. The dialing of the phone. The clattering of tea cups in the kitchen. The rumble of the man's voice, talking to the police.

He had moved down the hallway so slowly through that yellow glass; moving towards her in his stark suit, the gauze covering his face. Sitting there, with her limbs still jolting all over the place, she sees it over and over, as if on repeat: the white of his overalls crackling softly, his great masked face, moving towards her like an astronaut, heaving himself across the surface of the moon.

—

They took him away, the man with the knife.

He fetched the vinegar from the pantry for my mother, just as she'd asked. He took it out onto the deck for her.

The police found the bottle sitting out in the morning sun. They fingerprinted it, and they found him and took him away.

That was the end. And then there was the beginning, with him opening the kitchen door, and slipping inside, and pacing through the house, looking for her. She must have looked so pale when she appeared before him in the hallway, her breath catching in her throat—so pale and so clean, like something that could save him.

And then the lawn. The lawn, and her feet moving across it, faster and faster, pounding across the grass, leaping over the fence. The blue of her nightie slipping through the crack in the beekeeper's door, the swirl and hiccup of the fabric as she throws herself inside, slamming it shut behind her. And that man, bandana still over his face, hurrying through the house, back out onto the lawn, vinegar bottle in one hand, knife in the other, his frantic eyes searching for her across the grass, out over the hills, up into the sky; finding that she has flown away, that she is gone, that she is gone.

Panic

Greta and Mrs O'Brien are in an ambulance outside the Medical Centre.

'You have had a seizure!' the officer says to Mrs O'Brien, a little too loudly. He flicks his eyes over his checkboard, finds her name. 'Mrs O'Brien!' he calls. 'Can you hear me?'

She cannot, or perhaps she isn't listening. She lies, now, on the green vinyl bench where before she had sat. She had sat quite upright with her handbag on her lap, arms crossed over her chest, covering the buttons of her blue gingham shirt, the fabric bulging outwards slightly, displaying pockets of white skin underneath. In a soft American drawl she had said, 'The more the merrier.' Another patient was coming in the ambulance too. There would be three of them then: Greta buckled up on the stretcher; Mrs O'Brien on the bench opposite; one more.

The officer had squinted at them from the doorway.

'I reckon we can squeeze one more in,' he said, as if they were fillets of mackerel in a can.

Greta tried to nod at him brightly, though she didn't feel very bright at all.

Mrs O'Brien nodded too. 'The more the merrier,' she said, quite chirpily, and then she started.

It seemed like nothing at first, as if she was just cold or a little frightened, her eyes fixed on one spot on the wall, her body shivering all over. Then her neck flopped and her head started flapping around above her chest, her legs and arms going too. The wire-framed glasses she was wearing nearly took out an eye.

The officers took one end each and tried to hold her down. A slick of sweat covered her face, and her body seemed slippery too as it jerked around.

And then she stopped, dead still.

'You have had a seizure!' the officer says. His voice is tight, disapproving.

Mrs O'Brien's light blue eyes are like milk. She stares at the ceiling.

'Do you have epilepsy, Mrs O'Brien?' he calls. 'Do you *have* seizures?'

He grabs his clipboard and flicks through the pages. There is a Medic Alert bracelet on her wrist. He twists it towards himself, and frowns.

'Can you hear me, Mrs O'Brien?' he says. 'Hello?'

She doesn't look at him. She seems achingly calm, washed clean.

'Hello,' she says, as if she's just popped in for tea.

He smiles. 'Hello there,' he says. 'Good. What day is it, Mrs O'Brien?' He begins to feel for her pulse.

She hesitates and her eyes shift slightly from side to side.

'Sunday,' she says breezily.

'You have had a seizure, Mrs O'Brien,' he says. 'Do you know that?'

She turns her head and looks him right in the eye. Her voice sounds puzzled.

'I don't know *you*,' she says.

Outside is a dead autumn afternoon. Mrs O'Brien is right; it is Sunday, and even though they're in town, parked by After Hours, there is hardly anyone around. The doors of the ambulance are flung open. Mushy leaves fill the gutters. Cars roll by.

Greta tries hard to keep her breathing steady and she tries hard not to look at Mrs O'Brien. If she wasn't all buckled up she would get the hell out of here, she thinks. If she could walk, she would just get out.

'You *do* know me, Mrs O'Brien,' the officer is saying as if she's a stupid child. 'You were talking to me a few minutes ago.' His tone is incredulous. Then his voice lifts.

'What just happened?' he says. 'Do you know what just happened?'

Mrs O'Brien closes her eyes and makes a gurgling sound in her throat. One foot starts tapping against the vinyl.

'Here she goes again!' he says. He places his two hands firmly on her body.

Greta looks away, but on the polished white of the ambulance walls she can see the reflection of Mrs O'Brien's legs. They slice at the air. The whole vehicle shakes: a drum-beat played out by her limbs. When she looks back, one of Mrs O'Brien's trouser legs has ridden up, and the veins on her thick white calf seem to be pushing against the underside of her skin. A flap of stomach jiggles around like hard-set gravy.

The other patient appears at the ambulance door with an oxygen mask on, and then is bustled away. Greta holds tight to the edge of the blanket.

Over on the other side of the road she can see a motorbike shop, all closed up for the weekend, and beyond it a small hill with scrappy grass, a slice of sky. She counts to 10 in her head, and then back again: 8, 7, 6, 5 . . .

The shaking stops, abruptly.

'What's happening?' the officer says. 'You've just had two seizures in five minutes, Mrs O'Brien. What's going on?'

She makes a wordless gabbling sound, her mouth opening and shutting on her tongue, and then she bursts out from under his hands and, choking and gasping, throws herself out the ambulance doors into the white afternoon.

———

Mrs O'Brien is making a fool of herself out on the street in front of everyone. She screams and cries and tries to pummel the ambulance officer with her fists. She collapses into a seizure again, and then out again, and then in. Two police officers stop to try to help, and she wails at the top of her lungs.

'What have I done?' she cries. 'What have I *done*?'

Another ambulance comes, and they take her away.

'She doesn't have epilepsy,' one officer says to the other as they stand by the open doorway. He laughs almost bitterly. 'Panic attacks,' he says. '*Panic* attacks. That's what the Alert says. It's in her *head*.'

He runs his hands through his hair.

Mrs O'Brien had climbed on board and had said to Greta, 'An ambulance party!' and had said, 'The more the merrier,' quite happily, and then, Greta thinks, she just went under a wave. Just held her breath, and under she went.

*

Mrs O'Brien and Greta are in the corridor of the hospital. They are in their beds, lying on parallel sides, waiting to be seen. Mrs O'Brien's husband has arrived, and he stands by the bed, holding onto the bars on its side. Her black shiny handbag is slung over his sloping shoulder, and his head is large and flat like a squash racket.

Greta's mother has arrived too. She sips water out of a plastic cup.

'Imagine the poor man's life,' she says to Greta, so loudly the whole corridor must hear. 'Seizures caused by panic attacks? Whoever heard of such a thing?' She clacks her tongue.

Mr O'Brien does not talk to his wife and does not hold her hand. He holds so tightly to the metal bars that his knuckles are bone white. He seems dwarfed, like a child on the wrong side of his cot. His wife's flighty brown hair and moist head poke out from under the blankets, shuddering back and forth on the pillow.

The hospital staff come and go, dressed in their green plastic uniforms. The lights are bright with a yellow tinge. Doors swing open and shut again.

Mr O'Brien finds the water cooler, and begins trotting back and forth, the rubber from his small black shoes squeaking against the linoleum. He takes water to his wife like an animal might, almost senselessly trying to nudge her back to life. He tips the cup towards her mouth, and her juddering head knocks it, the water slopping out and over onto her neck. She doesn't seem to notice and he, undeterred, goes back for a refill.

Greta closes her eyes.

'They'll see you soon,' her mother says. 'Promise.'

But right now they are trying to talk to Mrs O'Brien.

'Do you know where you are?' a nurse asks. 'Are you listening?'

Mrs O'Brien's voice, light and soft as a child's, rises off the pillow.

'Truck,' she says hesitantly, as if it's the only word she knows. 'In a truck.'

'No, Mrs O'Brien,' the nurse says. 'You're in the hospital.'

Greta keeps her eyes closed, and senses the corridor as

something fluid, a body of water. The doors swishing back and forth, the rolling of wheels, the green-uniformed staff like pebbles being rushed along on a current. She and Mrs O'Brien have been struck dumb, she thinks. Stopped short in the middle of an ordinary day. They lie on opposite sides of the corridor, two bloated bodies washed up on the tide.

She can hear the squeaking of shoes going past her bed, and then the slow glugging of the water cooler. Mr O'Brien is going back for more, she realses. Helpless in the face of things, he's going back for more.

*

Two orderlies come, and they wheel Greta away. She counts the turns by watching the corners on the ceiling twist sharply above her. The orderlies' shoes squeak and the wheels hum; they are pushing her along, fast, as if she is a trolley in a race.

They wheel her into a booth, her own little room with an animal-print curtain, and her mother sitting beside her, holding her hand. Greta notices the dampness of it—her mother's hand, normally dry and strong—the slight pulse, deep under the skin.

'Look at the curtains!' her mother says. 'Do you think they're intended to appeal to the child within?'

Greta is only nineteen, but she doesn't know if they appeal to her child within, wherever she is. If she were here she would probably kick and scream, so she must be someplace else.

'Probably,' says Greta.

Her mother squeezes her hand supportively.

'What's that animal?' she says, pointing to something with spikes and a cartoon nose.

'An armadillo?' says Greta.

'Is it?'

'I think so.'

'Really?'

This could go on all day.

The doctor comes. He pulls up a chair, and sits down, and places one hand in the other. He tells Greta and her mother that they will have to do some tests. He says it as if it is neither a good nor bad thing; as if it is the thing he says over and over again, every day—which it probably is, of course. He has a tight, pointy face, and glasses propped right up against his eyes, but his body is lanky and relaxed, like a puppet, or Big Bird.

'So tell me again what happened,' he says.

'She collapsed,' says Greta's mother, 'in the doctor's surgery.'

'And you were at the doctor because of back pain?' he says to Greta.

'Yes,' say Greta and her mother at the same time.

'We're having trouble reading the doctor's writing on the notes,' he says. 'But it's kidneys. That's what we're thinking?'

'Yes,' says her mother. 'That's what the other doctor thought. That's what I think too.'

He turns to look at Greta's mother for the first time since he started talking, and pushes his glasses further up his nose—which doesn't seem possible—and he just looks at her for a moment, wondering, perhaps, where she's come from, how she got here. And then he nods, and smiles.

'We'll do some tests,' he says again, and gets up to leave.

And so that's what they do. *Tests.* They know nothing yet, they say, but the tests will tell them everything. All of them, the doctors, the nurses, Greta, her mother—they're all in the same boat; they're like children waiting to be taught how to spell; they don't *know* yet.

'I think we know as much as they do,' Greta's mother whispers to her. 'Maybe more.'

The tests begin. A nurse comes and collects blood. The little vials click as she does it. She takes Greta's blood pressure.

'Gosh,' she says brightly, 'isn't it low?'

'That's why she had to come in the ambulance,' Greta's mother says, quite assertively. 'It's so low she can't stand up!'

'Well, I guess that means you can't run away,' says the nurse.

'Yes,' says Greta. 'I would if I *could.*'

And they all laugh. Ha! Ha! Ha! Greta, too, although actually she meant it.

They need to do a urine test, the nurse says. 'This is going to be tricky!' She has a bright, bouncy ponytail and dark rings under her eyes. She and Greta's mother help Greta into a wheelchair and wheel her down another hallway. Greta's head lolls pathetically down by her chest.

She cannot control it; it is a disobedient dog. Her knees knock against each other, looking for support. She started the day like a normal girl—dressed, shoes on, hair done—and now she is just a jumble of bones and flesh, badly put together, unraveling round the edges like a piece of unfinished knitting. Her skirt rides up around her waist, and her cardigan is tucked in at the back, by mistake.

'Are you still with us?' says the nurse from behind.

Greta gives her the thumbs-up. Sure am.

When she's back in bed—the curtain pulled, her mother sitting beside her, expectantly, like someone waiting for a bus—the doctor comes to visit again. He has a stethoscope hanging round his neck. Under the fluorescent lights, a few hours gone by, he looks tired, his head small and pale like a peeled egg.

'So we're waiting for the test results,' he says, standing awkwardly by Greta's bed.

'You know nothing yet?' says Greta's mother.

'No. Not yet.'

He gives them a wavering smile.

'I want to do an ultra-sound though,' he says, 'to eliminate a few possibilities.'

'An ultra-sound?' says Greta's mother. 'Why?'

'Standard procedure,' he says. He smiles encouragingly at them again.

Greta suddenly imagines him getting out of bed, brushing his teeth, eating cereal, watching TV. She sees him as he is—just an ordinary, small-headed, rubbery-limbed man; almost a boy, really, despite his uniform and his stethoscope and the Dr in front of his name.

'An ultra-sound,' says Greta's mother when he's gone. 'How ridiculous.'

'What do you think it means?' says Greta, trying to keep the anxiousness at bay.

'Oh, they just like to play with their shiny new machines,' she says. But after she's said it, she pulls her lips in tight across her teeth and looks into the distance, as though she can see something there, far away.

Two orderlies come, skimming the curtain briskly back on its rail, undoing the locks on the wheels of Greta's bed.

'This one's off to Radiology?' they say to the room, themselves, each other: it's hard to tell which.

They wheel her off into the hallway, and then leave her there.

Greta's mother says she needs to go to the toilet. Her face wrinkles as she says it.

'What if they come and take you away while I'm gone?'

'Just go,' Greta says. 'I'll be fine.'

Her mother bustles off round the corner, one shoe squeaking desperately.

Greta lies looking up at the ceiling for what feels like a long time. Doctors and nurses fly past her and don't even look twice.

Far off, she can hear something wailing—is it a child or a woman? She would think it was an animal if she didn't know better. It ebbs, the sound—loud, soft, loud, soft—and then stops abruptly.

Greta holds her own hand, and looks down the corridor; wills her mother to appear around the corner. But she doesn't. Not at that moment. A small parade comes towards her instead—orderlies, a bed, someone trotting beside it.

It is Mr and Mrs O'Brien.

Well, Mr O'Brien, at least. Greta cannot see Mrs O'Brien at all. The blankets are pulled up tight over her chin, and she is lying still: just a hump under the fabric. Mr O'Brien trots beside the bed, keeping up like a dog on a leash. His enormous head jolts slightly as he walks; he's almost in a half run. His wife's black handbag is still slung over his shoulder—is simply a part of him now—and it swings rhythmically against his leg. He carries two plastic cups, one for himself, one presumably for Mrs O'Brien. He holds them purposefully, out in front of his body, like two trophies, keeping them steady so they don't spill.

Greta feels glad to see them.

She smiles and lifts her hand up in a half wave.

Mr O'Brien doesn't look at her. He doesn't look until he is right up close, passing right beside her bed. He turns his face towards her then, just for a moment. His hair is lifting off his forehead, as though he is walking into a head wind, but there is an expression of buoyant certainty on his face. He nods at Greta earnestly, holding the cups out in front of his chest as if to say—Don't worry. As if to say—Everything is under control.

History

I.

Lola is on the front porch, saying goodbye to Jack Wright.

The door is ajar behind her, and she leans against the edge of the frame. Jack shifts from side to side, and his eyes shift constantly too. But Lola feels calm, eerily calm, as if a disaster is about to strike, a huge wave perhaps, and she is ready for it. Ready to be dragged under by its great noise.

'Well, I guess we're all done,' Jack says to her, though he turns his head when he says it, out towards the street, the row of roofs, the potted palms by Mrs Jones's front door.

'Yes, Jack,' Lola says. 'That's right. All done.'

It is almost evening and the street lights are coming on all the way down Anderson Terrace. Traffic can be heard building up on Mayfair Road. Birds call out faintly, and Lola notices that the sky is a dull heavy grey, almost green, as it sinks down towards the roofs. That greyness is spreading, she thinks, up and out and down. Everything is getting darker.

Inside, Daisy is watching cartoons. Lola has given her an extra packet of chippies, to keep her quiet. She can hear nothing at all from the living room though. Not the tinny cartoon music or the sing-song voices—or the crackling of the chippie packet, for that matter. She wonders, vaguely, if Daisy might have slipped out the back door and wandered off somewhere down the street, perhaps with her small, square schoolbag on her back. She wonders this, but it hardly becomes a conscious thought, it is more like a soft pulsing in the back of her head, and she doesn't go and check, just stays there against the door frame, the hard of the wood between her shoulder blades.

Jack digs his hands deep into his pockets. He yawns, which is a sure sign that he's nervous.

'You and me,' he says, 'we could have made something of our lives together. Do you ever think that? That you and I could have made something?'

He says this to her chest, and Lola instinctively crosses her arms and breathes the smoke in the air, its slight sharpness moving through her nostrils and hitting the back of her throat.

'I think we made plenty,' she says, 'if that's what you mean.'

She'd intended for it to be funny—she meant, made plenty of love, made a big enough mess, that sort of thing. She thought he'd laugh, and then she could laugh too. They could laugh together and it would all feel okay. But Jack doesn't laugh, or even smile. He squints at the sky and at a plane's lights blinking across it. The sky is an inky blue now, flat and smooth as steel. She wonders if he heard her.

'Well, of course,' she says, 'of course I thought that once, Jack. But not any more. Why would I think that now? There's no point.' She can feel her voice rising, just a little. 'If there was a point, Jack, I would think it.'

He leans over and takes her fingers in his, inching his hand forward so that hers is soon totally swallowed. His palm presses against the tips. It is clammy, unnaturally so, Lola thinks, hardly warm at all. How odd, she thinks to herself, that they should end like this; him holding her hand so tight, sweating all over the place.

He says, 'The point, Lola, is that we're here, and we're talking. That is the point.'

His head shakes a little as he says it, a small tremor, and it reminds Lola of a musical instrument—the way the words have a slight lilt as they come out of his mouth.

*

Jack Wright had come over that morning, after Daisy had gone to school, and hadn't left all day.

That's not how it was supposed to be, but Lola had given up on trying to control things like that long ago.

Lola and Jack had sat in the front room and talked about

Jack's wife—now ex—and his kids, who were older than Daisy, the youngest in his first year of high school. Lola talked a little about Daisy too, but there was not so much to say, her being just little, and new to school. Jack feigned interest, but Lola could see the blankness in his face when she talked about Daisy, a blankness which he tried to cover up, quite unsuccessfully. She was not his child, after all. Why should he even pretend to care?

Jack had aged a bit, but in an odd way; some of him almost seemed younger. He appeared thinner and taller, wiry, and a little more stooped. His fingers constantly moved to the edges of his eyes, right by the temples, to rub the skin. He didn't seem to know he was doing this, which Lola thought was a bad sign.

He talked and talked—about all sorts of things, but mainly about his mother, who had just died; his mother, whom Lola hadn't seen for ten years. Lola hadn't seen Jack for a year or so either, as a matter of fact. He'd been out of town for a while; just dropped in every now and then to say hello quite out of the blue. But it was a different kind of hello this time. It was a bags packed, boxed up, plane waiting sort of hello. Jack's mother was dead, and he was off: that was the sort of hello it was.

The funeral had been two days before. Lola hadn't gone, but Jack told her all about it, whether she wanted to hear it or not. He stared off into space and told her how they'd put pointy shoes on her dead swollen feet, the sound the coffin made when they shut it. She'd looked as young as ever, he said. She'd had a boyfriend right up until the end—she'd *always* had boyfriends—and still dyed her hair blonde, though it was more like yellow. She had said to Jack on the phone, 'I think I may die this week, Jack,' casually, as if announcing the arrival of the mail. He had misunderstood; he thought she meant her hair, the roots.

Jack and Lola had eaten lunch at the table: spaghetti on toast, Jack's favourite. He pulled her towards him as she was walking past his chair; pulled quite firmly so that she stumbled a little, falling onto his knee.

'How long's it been, Lol?' he whispered into her neck. 'How long?'

'Jack, don't,' she said. 'You know we can't. Not now that you're going for good. Jack. Please.'

He burrowed his face deeper into the skin, but she could still hear his words, as if they were moving into the flesh, right into her, weaving up the inside of her throat, spiralling up the tunnels towards her ears.

'I always remember you, when I'm gone,' he said. 'Always, Lol, after we've been here. The scent of you.' His tongue flickered across her collarbone. 'The scent of you.'

He moved his hands squarely up under her dress, pressing the palms against her skin, his fingers searching around up there. She felt her head fall down towards his face, as if it wasn't hers any more, her own self slipping away. Her mouth was on his skin, and on his mouth, and inside it, her teeth grating a little against his gums and lips. She could taste the remnants of spaghetti in his mouth— that, and the taste of his skin, which was smoky, like a weak fire was trying to burn somewhere deep inside him, unable to really take light.

He was working at her dress with his hands, struggling with it, and the top was half off before it came back to her—a memory, or the reality of things—and she was able

129

to take a hold again. Jack had her bottom lip between his teeth. He was eating her alive.

'Jack,' she said, the word sounding slurred and poorly formed, hardly audible against his mouth. 'Jack, don't. Jack. Stop now.'

She pushed at his chin with her hand, and arched her head away, her neck on a strange slant, her face angled towards the window. She opened her eyes wide then. Out the window she could see the lemon tree in the back yard, its body heavy with fat yellow fruit. She just looked at it for a while, feeling the heaving of Jack's breathing all around her, but not listening to it, not paying attention. Jack's hands still moved against her skin, but slower now, one shoved awkwardly up under her dress—a stray finger hooked inside the elastic trim of her knickers—the other close to her neck, kneading at her, as if she were dough. Through the streakiness of the window the tree did not look as bright as it did from outside, but it seemed impossibly round, all those leaves and lemons forming one solid ball.

'The trouble,' Lola said, quite calmly, staring out the window, fixated on that tree, 'is that you only want me when you're not with me, Jack. That's the trouble.'

His hands went slack as she said it, the fingers seeming to recoil away from her skin. Lola felt as if she might cry, as if she could lose herself again, but in a different way. No. Not today. She'd done enough crying about Jack Wright to sink a ship—about him, and at him. She'd done enough of that.

She lifted herself up off his knee—up and away—and only half heard the exasperated sigh that came out of his mouth; only half heard it, she realised later, because he lifted his hands to his face as it slipped out. He knew she was right. What she'd said, he knew, was true.

He cleared the table, and they did the dishes, he humming softly to himself, pretending not to be cross. Afterwards they sat on the two-seater couch, side by side, not saying anything. Jack held Lola's hand and tried to put his arm round her shoulders, casually, but nervously, as if they were on their first date. His armpit smelt like someone familiar, she thought—the slight tang of sweat, the far-off smell of cheap deodorant hanging in the air—but it could have been the smell of anybody, really. She let herself be held by him, but she didn't respond; applied no pressure to his hand when he held hers, tilted her head slightly away when his arm curled round her neck.

They had not talked about it, his leaving, even though that was why he came around. They didn't talk about it all day, and they were only talking about it now because he was—leaving—and there were no two ways about that.

*

Lola sees that the sky is turning quite dark. There is still a yellowy sick kind of green above the horizon, but it is disappearing fast. The street lights are growing stronger, or that's how it seems. It is really just that the sky is giving up, she thinks; it is submitting to their electric glow.

Over the road Mrs Jones draws up in her car. Her terrier is sitting beside her in the passenger seat. Mrs Jones opens and shuts the doors, and talks to the dog as if it can understand every word. She can see Lola and Jack on the porch, but she doesn't wave. Her voice fades as she trots up the path, and then the sound disappears completely, punctuated by the slamming of the front door. Lights snap on inside.

They watch her draw the curtains.

'I would have liked to have gone to the Grand Canyon,' Jack says to Lola. 'Wouldn't you have liked to have gone there? I think of all the places to go that would be the one. Imagine, all that air, right down to the bottom where there used to be water.'

'You could still go there,' Lola says, quite sharply. 'Nothing's stopping you.'

'I could,' Jack says to her, and laughs, as if the thought has never occurred to him. 'Yeah, Lola, you're quite right.'

What a fool he is, she thinks to herself. A damn fool.

Overhead, a jet roars, making the whole porch shake. Jack watches it, waiting for it to pass, and then he claps his hands twice, in a brisk, energetic way. He is suddenly bright, as if he has just remembered how great he is in this world.

'Well,' he says. 'I guess this is me, then.'

He starts down the steps, and Lola moves along behind him, right down to the footpath and the road, right to his car.

Jack fumbles in his pockets for the keys, and pulls them out and unlocks the door; opens it. He stands before her, smiling a ridiculous jolly smile. He leans to kiss her cheek, and aims so far from her mouth that he hits her ear and the hair tucked behind it. He doesn't pause there, not even for a second.

He hops into the car, closes the door, winds down the

window. It squeaks, moving down in small jolts.

Lola has a sudden urge to burst his bubble. She hadn't intended to be nice, telling him he could still go to the Canyon on his own, but it seems to have given him a strange glow, as if he is already there, in the heat. She thinks of him booking a ticket and flying all that way, and driving in some snazzy car, a Cadillac probably, her Jack Wright, the wind blowing in his hair. She can see the cacti all around and the red parched earth, and the road, straight as far as you can see; him driving along it, fast, right to that hole in the ground.

She leans towards the window.

'You know what you said? About, do I ever think? I used to still think we'd eventually get married, until not so long ago. I kept on thinking that and believing it. That one day we would—' and then she pauses, moves her foot along the edge of the gutter. 'I thought that for a long time, Jack,' she says, 'but not any more.'

He turns the key in the ignition, and the headlights on, and the lights on the dashboard seem to spring towards his face, highlighting the creases round his mouth and eyes.

He smiles at her, though it almost seems a grimace, showing his gums which look a dark spongy pink, and the edges of the teeth below them, slightly stained.

'Lola Lollipop,' he says, smiling all the time. 'My little Lola Lollipop.' And then he accelerates, swerving out onto the road and away.

Lola pads up the steps and onto the porch and inside. Daisy is still there, sitting in the living room in the dark, the television flickering blue, making the whole room seem alive. Daisy's hands are in her lap and the whites of her eyes are lit up. She looks so small on that big puffy couch.

'It's dark,' Lola says to her. 'Why didn't you turn the light on?' And she flicks the switch so that the room is suddenly white, not flickering, not blue. How light swallows up darkness, Lola thinks, and the thought seems achingly meaningful, just for that moment, as if she's never thought anything like it before.

'Has Uncle Jack gone?' Daisy says.

'He isn't your uncle,' says Lola, 'but call him what you want. And yes, he has.'

She cooks dinner, and runs Daisy's bath, and makes her bed while she's splashing around in there. She empties out her schoolbag, finds her lunchbox and bins the remainders. The television is still going in the living room. She can hear the voices blaring down the hallway.

As she's drawing Daisy's curtains she looks out the window and sees Mrs Jones and the terrier in the front yard. Mrs Jones's outside light is on, so it looks as if the two of them are on a stage, the square of grass unnaturally green, the potted palms casting long shadows, the dog crouching, ears back, concentrating hard, looking slightly dismayed. Mrs Jones is congratulating it—though Lola can't hear the words, her tone is light and joyful, like bells—and fluttering her hands together. The dog is finished. It turns around and bounds inside. Mrs Jones pauses a moment in the cool autumn air.

*

At 9.15 the phone rings. It is Mike McDougall, Lola's boyfriend.

'Baby, baby, baby,' he says to her, and starts singing—the song about Lola, the one he always sings when he rings her up, as if she hasn't heard it a million times before. Does he know what it is about? Lola thinks. Does he realise the comparison isn't flattering?

She tries to make appreciative noises nevertheless, but she swings her slippered foot and examines the blunt, dark hairs sprouting on her legs.

Mike travels a lot, selling water filters to companies all over the country. He is calling from a motel. He is already in bed.

'Tell me about your day,' he says, once he's finished with his crooning. He yawns; she can hear him shifting in the sheets.

'My day?' Lola says naturally. 'You know. Daisy to school, Daisy home, Daisy to bed.'

'Yeah, Daisy,' Mike says. 'I called earlier. She said you were down on the road, saying goodbye to Uncle Jack.' He pauses, just for a second. 'Who's Uncle Jack?' he says. There isn't even a hint of suspicion in his voice.

Lola doesn't skip a beat.

'Oh you know,' she says. 'Jack Bauman? Have you met him? Jack Bauman, friend of Joyce's. Just dropped by. I'm not sure what for.' She can see a beetle moving across the floor. It may be a cockroach. She flicks her leg out to step on it, and then decides not to; sits back down.

'Jack Bauman? Doesn't ring a bell,' Mike says. He sounds weary. Lola hears him shift again in the sheets. 'Uncle Jack,' he says. 'I like that. Maybe Daisy should call me that—Uncle Mike, I mean. Uncle Mike. Good ring to it, don't you think?'

'Maybe she should,' Lola says. She feels a rushing in her blood, as if it's devouring itself, a cool swift crackling. She leans her cheek against the vinyl of the chair. 'I wish I was right there with you,' she says suddenly to Mike McDougall, lying in his motel bed somewhere in another town. She can picture his strong, leathery-skinned chest, the way his body narrows as it moves down towards the hips. She feels that she can almost see the view from his window, a red neon light flashing on and off, on and off. 'I wish I was right there,' she says to him again, in a voice she never uses. 'I wish I could crawl in beside you and lie with my head on your chest. Wouldn't that be nice? If we were lying there together?'

Mike sighs, or yawns, Lola can't tell which. He sounds pleased, though, as if the conversation is winding down, in just the right way.

'Yeah, doll,' he says to her. 'That'd be great. We could settle down and have a hell of a good sleep. Did I tell you I drove thirteen hours today?'

Lola is in the kitchen, cleaning up the dishes, when something makes her stop short. It is nearly ten o'clock and she thinks she's heard a strange noise, something from outside: that is how abruptly she stops to cock her head. She listens for a moment, but there is nothing. She's pretty sure of that. If she could see out the kitchen window she would be totally sure, but all she can see is herself, under the yellow kitchen light, strands of fly-away hair illuminated, standing up all over her head like a fuzzy halo. She looks tired and bag-eyed and saggy, and she just looks right into that reflection, not at the cupboards, or the calendar, or the cookbooks that are behind her, all reflected back too, but at her face, right into it.

The sound, she suddenly realises, is coming from inside her, seemingly far away, but inside her, definitely. Maybe the wave has hit, she thinks.

But it's not Jack. She doesn't think so anyway. She pictures him baring his teeth at her like a dog, just before he drove away; the way he said, Lola Lollipop. Lola Lollipop, as if she was eighteen again.

No, it wasn't Jack Wright and his leaving. He was a fool and she was glad.

She dips her hands back into the tepid water and swirls the dishcloth over a plate, slowly. The sound is still in there, a faint rushing, like a dam has broken and a river is moving through her body, up towards her head. She thinks of Mike McDougall, her man Mike, somewhere in a motel bed, snoring probably, his mouth wide open. Thinking of him makes her pause again. She lifts her head and looks at the yellow room on the window pane. It is as if the dark outside isn't really there. It is only her in this world, in this yellow room. She smiles, just to check, and sure enough her self smiles back, reassuringly.

She thinks about what she said to Mike on the phone. The surge that moved through her body when she said it. It had almost felt like happiness, that feeling, but not quite. It was power, Lola realises. The power to erase a whole day, and to erase any suspicions as well. How many times has she lied about Jack and never noticed it, that feeling? It was the power of sweetness; the conviction of it. It was still moving through her body, that power, filling her up.

And the astounding thing, Lola thinks, is that when she said those words—the ones about wanting to be with him, right there in his bed, her head on his chest—just at the moment they were coming out her mouth she actually believed them to be true.

She looks dead into her own eyes.

'Fool,' she says out loud, and the reflection says it back to her. And she doesn't just mean Jack Wright or Mike McDougall; she means herself too. Lola Jeffries. She feels suddenly sad for them, for all three of them.

She leans forward, bracing herself against the metal of the sink, up to her elbows in dishwater.

II.

Late one February afternoon, Jack called Lola at work—at the Riverside Tearooms—and said he was in town for the night and needed to see her. Urgently.

Lola said no.

This was seventeen years ago, at least. Long before Daisy. Long before Daisy's weed of a father, Trent Monroe. Long before Mike McDougall and the monotonous drone of his voice.

—

She had looked down at her hands and listened to the sound of Jack's breathing coming down the line. 'Please,' he said, 'Lol, please.' And then he had paused. 'Come on,' he said, 'please.'

She said no again. There was a long silence. Maybe she didn't sound like she meant it, not really, because on the third please she said okay, and he didn't seem surprised at all.

'Give me your number at the motel,' she said, looking out the window at people hurrying by on the pavement below. 'So if I change my mind I can call.'

'Nope,' Jack said. 'You won't change your mind. It'll be fine, Lola. Promise.'

She had walked home in the early evening sun, and lay on her unmade bed, looking up at the ceiling. All the windows were closed, shutting out the sound of the cars. Her clock ticked loudly beside her head. In the next room the phone rang three times, and then stopped. She should have a shower, she thought. Change her clothes. Put some foundation round her eyes, which she'd noticed recently had developed blue rings the colour of a dull, hazy sky. She was only twenty-three—too young, she thought, for signs of weariness like that.

Get ready, she said to herself out loud.

But she just lay there, looking up. Quite still.

Jack Wright had taken advantage of her innocence, if the truth be told. That's not how she'd seen it at the time, but retrospect had put a fresh film on things. She'd met him when she was eighteen, he pushing thirty, and then left him two years later. She hadn't seen him or heard from him since.

There had been an incident, of course. A long line of them, and then—what was the saying?—the straw that broke the camel's back. Jack, picking her up from the bus stop one night after she had been away for a week visiting home. The dead look in his eyes. The way he told her, casually, just what he'd been doing while she was gone.

They were driving down the dusty road, the night sky glowing a strange yellow above the houses, and as they turned a corner Jack said, staring straight ahead the whole time, 'I gotta tell you, Lola. I've gone bad.'

She had almost laughed out loud, imagining him as something in the fridge, something overdue for the bin. She kept her hand on his knee, resting lightly as it had been before, and looked out through the windscreen at the patch of road lurching into view, each illuminated square the same as the next, and said, 'Really?'

She felt that if she lifted her hand, even her finger, off his leg, something irreversible would happen. A crumbling of sorts; a slow unravelling.

Jack kept his eyes on the road and his hands on the wheel.

'I've been drinking again,' he said calmly. 'And taking drugs. And sleeping with women.'

Lola moved her tongue round the inside of her teeth.

'Have you, Jack?' she said.

'I have.'

They drove on, the lights from the dashboard lilting

up towards their faces. Lola watched the clock flick from 8.11 to 8.12 to 8.13, and then she picked up her arm—that's how it felt, as if she was picking it up like a kitten, or a small doll—and placed the other hand in her lap, one palm resting on top of the other.

'Are you sorry?' she said, achingly calm.

'Well, yes,' he said, 'and no. No use crying over spilt milk, I figure.'

He took another corner, and then another, and pulled up behind their flat.

Lola got out and shut the door and walked quickly across the tarmac, feeling the air brushing against her face. She could hear the boot opening and shutting; Jack getting out her bags, the satchel of preserves her aunt had palmed off on her, along with mouldy lemons and shelled peas. He moved up the stairs behind her, weighted down, and set her bags on the floor in the kitchen.

He looked at her wearily.

'I didn't mean it as anything,' he had said. 'You know that. Let's just put it behind us, hey?'

*

Lola ate a piece of toast and walked twenty minutes across town to meet Jack at the motel down by the river.

She had showered for longer than usual, scrubbed at her scalp to try to remove the smell of Sheryl's steaks that always hung around on her hair. She had done it up into a sort of a casual pile on the top of her head—her hair—and sprayed at it profusely. That would help with the smell too, she thought. Somehow, since she last saw Jack (was someone playing some kind of crazy trick on her?) crow's feet had begun snaking their way towards her temples, and there was an incipient sag around her waist.

People were wandering home, carrying shopping bags on their arms, wearing light sweatshirts and skirts and shorts. They talked quietly to one another. Some walked alone, heads down. It would not be dark for a while yet.

Jack was waiting at the motel entrance, leaning casually against the fence.

'You came,' he said to her, perhaps trying to hide the victorious curl of his lip, but not succeeding in doing so. He was wearing pale jeans, worn jandals, one of which he'd discarded on the grass. He was tanned, more so than Lola had ever seen him. She had put a dress on, garishly coloured, its fabric almost transparent. She suddenly wished she hadn't.

'Did you think I wouldn't?' she said. 'Did you really think I wouldn't?'

He started towards her with more purpose than she could ever turn from, reaching out his arms.

'I hoped that you would,' he said.

She had felt flooded with an almost appalling relief. It could have knocked her backwards, that flood. Yes—a happiness so close to despair.

Jack's room smelt musty, even though all of the windows were open, letting in the river air. They drank sherry out of plastic cups, and Lola watched—remembered—the way Jack's hands moved when he smiled at her, his fingertips always framing his face, pale moons under the nails.

He leaned over, touched his thumb to her mouth.

'There you are,' he said.

And before Lola could stop him—before she could even pretend to object—he was on the floor, starting at her toes, working his way upwards. He licked at her fingertips, and at the skin behind her knees.

He said, 'All I've thought about for three years is getting you into bed.'

She shook her head, laughed; but she did believe him. She believed him—almost—completely.

'And how do we get these off?' he said to her, or rather to her underwear.

Afterwards Jack said to her, quite out of the blue, 'Well, I'm sorry for all the trouble I've caused you.'

They were sitting on the bed, their backs pressed hard against the wall, getting their breathing back to normal.

'You've always been too good for me, Lol,' he said. 'Everyone always said so. I know that.' He didn't look at her as he said this. The words were directed straight out in front of him, and their bodies weren't touching at all, just sitting side by side, like the bodies of strangers on a bus.

'What I wanted to tell you,' Jack said, and he reached out his hand to her as he said it, though his eyes stayed fixed, looking hard at the cupboards on the opposite wall, 'is that I got a girl knocked up, and I'll have to marry her, I guess.'

Lola was looking at her thighs as he said this—the stickiness of them high up, the insides of them covered in a transparent slick. Her veins were pressed right up against the skin so that the colour of them—her thighs—was too pink, nearly purple.

Jack yawned.

'I'd probably rather marry you,' he said.

He squeezed her hand, and then let go.

Out of the window, the river looked lazy, a muddy brown, hardly moving at all. Was it the smell of the river that Lola could taste in her mouth, or was it Jack? She leaned across to her half-filled plastic cup and spat into it. The spit wormed around in there for a moment, all white and frothy, and then rose to the top. Lola licked at her lips. The taste was still there. It was Jack, for sure.

'I'd probably rather marry you,' Jack said again, monotonously, as if she hadn't heard the first time.

Lola began to laugh, an awful breathless laugh, like a wheeze.

'Should I take that as a compliment?' she said, though the words sounded more like the far-off screech of a bird. 'Jack? Should I be *glad*?'

'I guess I just thought you should know,' Jack Wright said to her, though his voice now sounded defeated. Lola saw out of the corner of her eye that he was searching for his jeans and, once he found them, through the pockets. Looking for his fags.

The best way out—or so it seemed at the time—was across the river.

Later, Lola wondered why she had thought this when, really, walking out through the gates of the motel and down the road would have been the simplest way home. Maybe she was half drunk, from the sherry.

It was beginning to get dark, and the sky, down low by the hills, was a dirty red. Lola had her dress back on, but somehow had forgotten her sandals. She was damned if she was going to go back for them.

It was simple—she would swim. Jack couldn't swim to save himself, or so he said.

Lola could see the milky light shining out through the open window of his room. It was not dark enough to seem strong, yet. It looked weak, washed out. Jack, she imagined, would be in there drinking himself into a stupor. Though perhaps part of her thought—part of her hoped—he might just come out across the perfectly groomed lawn and stand there on the bank, helpless, watching her swim away. That would have been nice.

The water was not as warm as she expected, and it was filled with silt. Lola didn't care. Not about the muddiness, the possibility of eels, or her dress which was billowing around her like a sail. She'd swum in the river before, though never all the way across. If she concentrated, she would make it to the other side in no time. It wasn't hard.

Jack had taken her head in his hands, palms against the base of her neck, holding her like someone might hold a new baby. That's what he'd done as he was lying her down. He'd held her head like that, looking at her as if she was something astonishing; something unexpected that he'd found on the bottom of a lake. Lola couldn't get away from it, that moment. The heat of his hands seeping right into her skull. She shook her head—no—every time it came back to her.

145

The sky grew dark quickly. It happened faster than she expected. She was already halfway across, although she was slowing herself down by turning round to look for Jack every once in a while. She thought she saw him against the motel lights, coming across the lawn, his shadow stretching out in front of him, but when she looked harder she saw it was only a woman in a short skirt and oversized teeshirt. Jack's light was still on, anyway, and when she turned to look again the curtains were drawn. He was still in there, for sure.

The red on the horizon had all but disappeared. It had been replaced by a deep blue, an indigo blue. Was that the word for it? It was almost impossible to tell where the hills ended and the sky began. Lola began to tread water, just to rest for a while. She would have to conserve energy to keep her strength up, even though she was a good swimmer. She had heard once about a man who went far out into the sea, so far that he couldn't possibly make it all the way back, on purpose. She would not want anyone ever to think she had done that.

The sound of voices moved across the water towards her. Perhaps they were coming from the playground in the motel's grounds. They did sound like children's voices, high and song-like. She would not allow herself to turn around and look for them, though—to look for those voices. From now on she would not allow herself to look back at the motel at all.

Things with Jack Wright were over, Lola decided. She was done with him. She would swim to the other side, and then she would run home, barefoot but fine despite that. Despite all of it. She would run to dry herself out—and

Jack Wright and the sediment of him all over her skin, inside and out, would fly right off her, right out of her.

'I'm done with you,' she said to the dark sway of grass on the bank, her legs beating beneath her, head turned away from the motel and its grounds, away from Jack and his curtained window.

'Do you hear that?' she called, though who she was saying it to she really didn't know.

The memory—that small contraction in her chest—of Jack on the bed, looking down at her, tried to slide back into her head, but she shook it out. Jack was a nuisance in her life—that's what he was—and she would brush him away, like soot.

Yes, Lola thought, and her body felt suddenly light, buoyant in the river. She was done with him, and everything would be just fine. She was sure of it. Jack Wright—he was nothing but history.

Relief

In July the lawyer phoned to say the charges had been dropped. The girl hadn't changed her story, he said, but had decided she wanted to put it all behind her, get on with her life.

Judy took the call. After she had hung up she sat down heavily on the settee and cried a little, though in a gulping self-conscious way, as if the relief was something she had to paste over herself, like a glaze. She tried Don's phone—as the lawyer had said he had done—but it was indeed out of range, and so she left a message asking him to call.

Later, when she talked about that moment, she described

herself falling back onto the sofa as if hit by an invisible force. It was the relief that did it, she said. It had knocked her off her feet. A palpable presence in the room.

Don worked in accountancy, though he hadn't always done so. For years he'd taught maths at the local high school, but everyone felt it was best if he gave up his position, given the circumstances. No one wanted to kick a man when he was down, Don's boss had said, so a friend of a friend had arranged for an interview at a small accountancy firm in the suburbs. There were only six other employees, and they were all men. Males would be more sympathetic about such things, the principal had said—including himself in the generalisation—but they really couldn't keep him on there, especially with the risk of it getting out amongst the students.

Don had gone willingly, afraid of that himself. He had already felt that young women were looking at him differently. Or was it just his imagination. Surely they couldn't have heard the rumours at that point.

Somehow Don had always known inside himself that it would never go to court. He'd willed that; wouldn't allow himself to imagine anything else. That's why he felt nothing much when Judy called, and then called again, and then finally got a hold of him once he was back at the office. He looked up from his desk as she spoke, his eyes searching outside the window.

Nothing unusual was happening out there.

*

On Sundays Don sometimes went to church with Judy and her husband Clive, even though he—Don—wasn't a believer. Judy and Clive had been his everything since the accusations, and he almost felt that he was doing his penance, accompanying them as he did. They were liberal Presbyterians—that's how they described themselves— but Don found the atmosphere of the church oppressive. Liberal Presbyterian seemed a contradiction in terms to him.

It was odd how a person could become something they never would have wanted to be. Judy had been wild during their childhood and adolescence, sometimes vaguely frightening. That's what came from being the only girl of three boys, he thought. She'd been gay for a while, in her late teens; and had then grown her hair so long she could sit on it, had dressed in faded kaftans. She had settled into middle age now, though—her hair in a blonde tidy bob, a collection of Venetian glass in a cabinet in the lounge. She was reliable-seeming. And she had been more than reliable for Don. She had taken on his battle as if it were her own. A war between darkness and light—those were the words she used to describe it. She used language like that when she was fueled up on red wine.

It was Judy and Clive who got the lawyer involved early on. Judy and Clive who helped cover the costs. It was important to try to keep it all quiet. Don knew that as well as they did. Once something like that got around, you'd spend the rest of your life trying to get the stain out.

*

Judy talked to her sister-in-law, Cherie, regularly on the phone. Judy worked four days a week, Monday to Thursday, in the archives section of the National Library. Friday was the day she set aside for herself, for catching up on things. Cherie and Michael had a large block of land—nobody could say *they* didn't work hard—but in the middle of the day Cherie normally took some time out. She had been married to Michael for twenty-two years—she really was just part of the family. If the truth be told, Judy needed her support. She often found herself feeling bewildered and anxious—standing in the queue at the train station, searching for something in the supermarket, finding herself in a room she'd gone into for something and not knowing what that something was. The stress, everybody agreed, had been unbearable. That girl would be responsible for putting them all in early graves, Cherie said. What a thing to have on your conscience! She had laughed when she said it, but any humour they tried to bring to the situation always felt forced and hollow. Unsurprising, of course—with all things considered.

On the Friday following the call from the lawyer, Judy called Cherie earlier than usual. It wasn't even close to lunchtime, and she expected Cherie not to answer, being out and about, most probably tending the land—but she felt a certain agitation, and Clive, whom she'd already tried, was in a meeting. It was adrenalin, or something. She couldn't settle herself down.

Cherie did answer. She sounded breathless, having hurried inside to get out of the rain. She told some long anecdote about one of the cows. Judy didn't have the energy for it.

'And how's everything there?' Cherie said. 'How's Don?'

Judy walked to the window, leaned against it, rubbed at a little streak with the edge of her shirt. 'You know what he's like,' she said. 'Hard to read.'

'It probably hasn't even sunk in yet. I can hardly believe it's over myself.' Cherie was doing something—busy—her voice coming down the phone in jagged little puffs.

Even though Cherie and Michael lived four hours away, the rain was travelling. Insubstantial drops spattered the courtyard. Judy noticed that one of the fabric deckchairs wasn't on a tilt. A pool would form on its seat.

'I'll write Paula another letter,' Judy said. 'I've already decided. She has to be told. The impact this has had on all of us. It's god damn near ruined our lives.' She felt her energy lift then, a soaring feeling, like she could take off.

And then the conversation dropped—or lifted—into its familiar territory. The details had an electric charge—of *course* they did—a charge that made Judy feel sluggish unless she was able to let it all out. These conversations with Cherie always left her feeling exhausted, but it was a peculiar kind of exhaustion, tinged with a faint euphoria.

'I mean, she always had it in for him. Don't you think? Even in the early days, when I look back now, she wanted to bring him down. She's a genius of disguise, Paula. She had us all fooled.'

'For years,' Cherie said. 'We were fooled by her for years.'

'And to use her daughter like that. A pawn in her game.

Don took her on as if she were his own—and that's not easy with adolescents. And, now, for her to say that he did that to her—' Judy exhaled audibly, started tidying piles of things on the table— 'even if it supposedly happened when everything was falling apart. Don! Doing something like *that* to a *girl*. It's laughable.'

The rain got heavier—a sudden downpour, little bits of hail in it bouncing around the courtyard. The cloud had enveloped everything.

'What I don't get,' Cherie said. 'Let's say it was true— why she would have waited eight bloody years to say anything about it? Eight years. With a secret like that!'

'It's not true,' said Judy. 'That's why it took so long. There was no secret. Only fabrication.' She felt all filled up with the relief of it, this conversation.

Here is sanity, she thought to herself. This is what is sane.

*

The rain started falling and didn't stop for weeks. It felt as if the heavens had opened and then forgotten how to close again. Doors and windows became swollen in their frames, wouldn't open properly. The gutters by the road roared like little rivers.

Don started walking everywhere in the rain, even though his shoes filled up with it and squelched. He felt easier, out there in the rain. He was fifty-four years old, living in a house too big for just one person, now mortgaged to the hilt. Spending whole weekends with his sister and her husband as if they were his only friends. He told himself that it was because they lived just around the corner in their recently acquired house; that it was more to do with a sort of practicality than anything else. Maybe that was true.

Sometimes he thought he saw the girl, going by on the bus, an indistinct figure through the window. It had been ten years since Paula had left him, taking her too. She was in her early twenties now—he knew that exactly, from seeing the statements his lawyer had given him to read. Twenty-four.

He would think it was her, but it never was—only a flash of something—and his eyes scanned rooms, supermarket aisles, streets, in a sort of resigned panic, an alertness, really, that she might turn a corner and suddenly be right there in front of him. When he'd first got wind of the allegations, he'd searched cars, standing at the pedestrian crossing, watching out for the two of them—Paula and her. He imagined at the time that he might go right up to the passenger window, catch her eyes, shake his head, perhaps mouth No at her. *No.*

He had heard she had a nervous breakdown a couple of years before the allegations all came out. He had suffered— he realised now—something like that in the time Paula was leaving him. He knew what it was like when the world folded in on itself in that way. An oiliness—an oil slick— covering everything.

*

Judy wished she had never read the statements—what Don had supposedly done. The details had gone into her subconscious—with details as bad as that, how could they go anywhere else?—and she dreamt about things she had never dreamt about before. There were small blades that cut at skin that lay like a carpet all over the floor. Or Don running away from her down the street, carrying an enormous bag that she saw, when she got closer, had wisps of long dark hair flying out through a tiny hole, strands of it caught in the zip. Or visiting Don at night, and the rooms of his house all changed around, every closed door leading to a bathroom, and Don's voice suddenly behind her, saying, Don't go in there; her turning and seeing him looking back at her, so tired-seeming—the tiredness the most frightening thing of all.

Don't go in there.

Or a scratching at the back door, the sound like something a possum might make. Irregular, but insistent. Opening it, and Don lying there, or sometimes the girl—looking young, and bony kneed, the age she would have been—always in a mess, always whispering something that sounded like *he*. Lifting her head towards Judy. A hole in her neck where the throat should be.

She mentioned them to the minister but no one else. It was natural, he said, in times of great stress to have dreams that inhabited the realm of darkness. He seemed unconcerned by them, almost not to hear her. They were only dreams. That girl, and her lies, had got inside Judy's head, that's all. They tainted the day only slightly. Just a little smudge in its corner.

Early on—when it had all first come out—Judy had gone to visit Paula, knocked on the door, tried to talk some sense into her. Paula had stayed calm. Judy hadn't. It was this calm assuredness that Paula used to get people onside, to confuse them. She blamed herself, she said to Judy. Things had been bad between her and Don. He knew she was trying to leave. He was unwell. Very unwell. But she had had to keep travelling with her job. What else could she do? She had left her daughter behind with him a few nights every fortnight. That's when it had happened. It never occurred to her that he would do that. Not for an instant.

The signs had been there all along, she had said— that something was terribly wrong—but it had taken her years to piece things together. Her daughter had been on sedatives for years to help her sleep. Was unable to go anywhere by herself at night. Fainted, once, in a room full of people when someone mentioned Don's name.

Judy had felt her breathing get tight, high in her chest, a feeling she imagined asthma to be like. She had raised her voice—the wrong thing to do. It hadn't made their cause look any better. But Don was her brother. She loved him. There had been too much loss. Too much loss in his life already.

*

A year or so after Paula left him, a woman Don was seeing had taken him to a bar in a new city—a city he'd never been to before. The bar was underground, below the level of the street, and the heat in there was alarming. The music was too loud. There were too many people. Low-hanging lights were knocked at by heads and erratically waving arms. It was like coming upon an ancient war ritual—all those violently throbbing bodies, leaping up and down, doing something that was presumably supposed to resemble dancing.

'I feel like I've been here before,' Don had said—or rather yelled—to his date.

'What?'

'I feel like I've been here before.'

She looked at him and shook her head, seemingly unsure if he was joking or not, perhaps unable to decipher his words. The city was totally new to him. He had told her that over and over again. She was introducing him to it, his tour guide. He could tell from her weary expression that often he didn't make sense to her.

Don had watched Suzie, or whatever her name was, become absorbed into the mass, sucked under like someone being dragged underwater. A few minutes later she returned—for him. He stumbled into the crowd behind her.

The dancing bodies had thrashed all around him. Animals: a man beside him twisting violently, like a snake. Don's head was making a sound like a jet, the screech of its wheels braking against tarmac. Could anybody else hear it? Was the sound coming out of his mouth? He fought his way out of there. Up the stairs. Outside.

That was the first time he had experienced it outside of the house. It had been happening, occasionally, for months before that, but only when he got up at night. There was something about the darkness of the hallway, the sound of his footsteps shuffling down it, the dull light from the streetlamp outside the toilet window that made his skin look grey. The closed door, when all the lights were out, and then the sound of it, the shushing sound, opening across the carpet.

Two years ago he had been the first person to arrive at the scene of a car crash. A girl had gone through the windscreen, her hands up to her face. The bones of her knuckles were showing through like a set of large rounded teeth emerging out of wound-red gums. Her face was not too bad, but her internal injuries were critical—though Don didn't know that at the time. When he arrived she had managed to get herself up off the road, and was moving in circles—a sort of a half run, almost a skip—that looked appallingly helpless, inappropriately comic. He managed to get her to lie back down on his coat on the road, tore his shirt up to try to bandage her hands. She was young, perhaps in her late teens, and once she was down she became subdued, distant. She didn't respond to his questions, but made a sound in the base of her throat, not really a crying sound, but something worse than a whimper. Her fingers were still able to move, and she tapped them against her chest, repetitively, a heartbeat on the wrong side. Was she trying to remind it—her heart—what it needed to do? She seemed to be desperately trying to calm herself. He talked to her about his day, where he'd been, what he'd done, trying to remain calm too. Bangles, greased with blood, jangled on her arm.

Later, after the ambulance had arrived—after they had lost her—Don drove home without his coat and shirt, and even then still speckled with her blood. That echo had sounded as he was stepping into the shower. The smell of her, when he had got up close—not the smell of blood, but something else, every time she moved. It was sweat, but more than that. A smell like one of those bugs—was it called a stink beetle?—radiating panic. It was unmistakable. The recognition entered his body, sharp that time, then lurched away.

*

Judy and Clive organised a dinner to celebrate Don's freedom. Cherie and Michael drove down from up north, and the five of them drank wine and ate homemade pizzas. Judy made one of her specialty cheesecakes, adorned with chocolate truffles from the deli down the road. Don made jokes about not wanting to be the centre of attention, and he seemed weary to her, somehow distant. He was like that—hard to read, hard to understand. He'd always been complicated.

'To innocence!' Clive said, raising his glass to him.

'To innocence!' he responded, his voice in a chorus with the rest of the room.

He had walked over in the rain, and his woollen jersey and worn leather shoes were giving off an odour like wet dog. When Judy sat down next to him it was almost overpowering. When had he last washed properly? His taupe-coloured pants were fringed with grey around the edges of the pockets, and the bottoms were soggy, quite black with dirt. His teeth, she noticed, seemed more stained than usual, the colour of old people's toenails when they grew too long. They'd been yellow for years, his teeth, but they were definitely getting worse.

'The truth will always out!' said Michael, red-faced and growing drunker by the minute, raising his glass again.

'To the truth,' they all said, smiling at each other. It was time for more cheesecake, and possibly a little more whipped cream. Everything was turning out all right. The trauma of it all would leave them soon.

Judy had first heard about the allegations from Paula, who called her one day, steady-voiced but a little breathy, her voice growing low at times, quite deep. Someone in the family needed to be told, she had said, and Judy was the obvious choice, living close by, and being closer to Don than anyone. Her daughter had decided to lay a formal complaint with the police. Don would certainly need some support.

Don, whom she'd gone to see afterwards, seemed resigned, his movements unusually measured. He laughed every now and then, and shook his head, like a man who had misplaced something and was bewildered and slightly ashamed at having done so. She, on the other hand, felt enraged, a terrible tension vibrating in her knees. Don was a good man—she told him—a fine schoolteacher; a fair person; kind. He was a good person. Good and kind. An innocent man. He looked mostly at his hands as she spoke, but she knew he was listening.

It was only at the end of their conversation that she questioned him. She did ask him if he had ever done anything wrong. She gave him the opportunity to say it was true, even though she believed completely that it wasn't.

'I never laid a finger on her,' he said, and it was only then that his movements seemed to become agitated, his fingers rolling a piece of tissue into a little ball, then moving it from palm to palm as if it was hot. A little bubble of spit had gathered in the corner of his mouth as he'd said it. It had grown bigger, moved across his lip as he spoke, dribbled a little down his chin. Had she been too hard on him? She felt sick about it to her stomach. Of course he hadn't done it. Of course not. When she got home she called him to apologise.

The first of her bad dreams came not long after that. Judy and Don were sitting in a bedroom, sitting beside a bed that had a girl in it, although Judy couldn't see her face. The two of them were talking about ordinary things—their parents and siblings, Judy's job, the books they'd recently read. The girl was not alive, and they both knew that. It didn't seem strange, at the time, that her body was moving a little under the covers. Her dark hair was slicked back, gluey-looking and wet. Don seemed so undisturbed by her presence—quite happy—that Judy felt calm, undisturbed also. She looked at her watch, and realised she was late. I have to go! she said. He got up to let her out. As he was closing the front door, she caught his smile, wide mouthed, and gummy. It was like a baby's, his mouth, though the gums were dark, not fresh and pink like a baby's would be. And no teeth in it. No teeth at all.

*

It had rained almost solidly for over a month. Don didn't mind it like everyone else seemed to. He liked the way it soaked through his coat, jersey, shirt, right to the skin; the little squelch that it formed between the insoles of his shoes and feet. It found its way into everything.

Sometimes, when he was walking home, he felt an urge to turn off two blocks earlier, to turn into Judy's street, walk through the gate and up the path and in through the front door without knocking. The impulse would start at his feet and ripple up through his body, like applause. The rain seemed to make the desire stronger, but it had actually started long before the downpours. It would come upon him, but if he ignored it and kept walking it would fade away soon enough.

When he was a boy he had taken his mother's engagement ring from the box on her dresser, and had gone down to Pryor's field to show it to a girl who was pretty but had a lisp when she spoke. He put it in his pocket, and hopped some of the way, and when he arrived there, at their meeting place, it was gone. He searched, quite desperately, while the lispy-lipped girl watched, her arms folded across her flat chest. It wasn't anywhere. And the grasses were so tall and dry, scratchy like tussock. He returned home, defeated in every way, a faint high-pitched note sounding in his ears.

There had been a burglary, his mother said. A crime. He heard her, that evening, talking on the phone to the police. For weeks he still searched for it, every afternoon after school—down on his hands and knees, trying to propel his way through the grass smoothly, as if it were water. And every afternoon he would return empty handed, unable to avoid her presence—brusquely folding washing at the kitchen table, preparing dinner, the radio crackling in the background. Once he moved towards her—the possibility of saying those words pulsing in his throat—but when she turned towards him her expression seemed to prevent him from saying them. *It was me. Who took it. Me, who lost it.* Her face was so vacant, and that vacancy—that lack of suspicion—exonerated him. The relief was weighty, like a pendulum swinging inside him. If she didn't suspect him, somehow it seemed that it wasn't even true.

Don never turned down Judy's street on the days when he hadn't been invited. He kept walking, the rain staining his coat a darker blue, forming patches that eventually joined up, swamping him. Sometimes he rescued worms from the gutters down his street. He watched out for them, hooked them out of the water, laid them on the grass, crouched down to watch the way they jerked and flailed about: rescued but exposed. *It was me, who took it.* The relief of saying those words to her would have consumed him, he was sure of that. He would have been absorbed into the afternoon light, eaten up by it. His body, in the sunshine, dissipating like a cloud of dust.

The Dress

I don't remember the year Helen Davies came to school.
I imagine she might have been there all along, skirting
just on the margins of my attention. But when I look back
it seems that one day, suddenly, she was there. She had
probably been in my class all year—and maybe, even,
the year before that—but for one reason or another she
had been an insignificance; something neither wanted nor
disliked.

The first thing I remember of Helen is her standing in
the quadrangle with her brother, who was probably a year
or two older than us, maybe ten or eleven at the time. It

seems to me now that they could have just dropped out of the sky, so sudden is their appearance in my mind, and at the same time that they could have been there all along, waiting patiently for me to see them. They were standing right by the hop-scotch corner, which was empty, possibly *because* they were there, both with small crust-less sandwiches in their hands. They did not seem to be talking or eating, just standing there, staring at the numbered squares, but not hopping, and not looking sad either, as far as I could tell.

Helen was wearing a grey and pink striped cotton-knit dress with a slim tie round the waist, and even though it was not particularly pretty, and not new-looking at all, I looked at her and wanted it—that dress—and therefore wanted to know her, or notice her at least.

Helen and Simon Davies lived somewhere just out of town, and walked to and from school every day, together, which was rare. Most of us were dropped off and picked up by our parents, and a few came on the school bus, but no one other than Helen and Simon walked. Even though Simon was older than us, he wasn't in the oldest class at school, but he looked like he should have been, stretching out of his clothes and skin like a malignant growth, out of control. He towered over Helen, his meaty hands, arms and legs thick and slightly grotesque; his head large and lumpy like a sprouting potato. Next to him Helen looked like something that could have been blown in on a high wind. She was small and narrow, with olive, almost dirty-looking skin, and a cloud of short brown hair, always greasy at the roots but fluffy everywhere else, quite soft-looking, like cotton wool. From far off, her head looked like it had been caught up in a whirl of dust—a round, earthy tornado—so indistinct was the line between her hair and the air around it.

The two of them—Helen and Simon—were odd together, but somehow seemed to operate as one: two opposing ends of the spectrum, beauty and the beast, though Helen could hardly have been called a beauty, really, at all. But it was the quality they had, like characters who had just stepped out of a fairy tale or a myth, eternally chained together, ethereal and world weary in a painfully ordinary sort of way.

At some point, after I first noticed them—or first *remember* noticing them—everyone else seemed to notice them too. A morbid fascination developed, rippling through our class and the entire school. Helen kept out of everyone's way, sitting quietly at the back of class, but all of a sudden she carried with her a certain mystique. Nobody in our class had ever paid attention to Simon, who was simply older than us, and ugly; too big and overbearing to be picked on. But he began to draw attention to himself, and because the bigger kids just ignored him, we were more than happy to comply. We began to call him Simple Simon, though I don't think any of us knew what it meant. It would make him go into an instant rage, lumbering around the playground, his flubbery lips sending out showers of spit, him sort of laughing to himself, hysterically, despite the stumbling and the fury. We all found it exhilarating—this reaction—and would squeal and coo, scattering ourselves around the playground. Helen wouldn't move or make a sound. She stood or sat somewhere on the edge of it all, watching and yet not watching; waiting for him to stop.

Sometime nearing the end of that year my two best friends, Rachel and Myra, started to slip out of my grasp. Myra had been premature as a baby, and had something wrong with her lungs, and she got sick at some point in that year, and was in and out of hospital, in and out of school. She had been the glue that stuck the three of us together, and Rachel suddenly didn't want to play with me any more, at morning tea or lunch. It was not that I was alone or entirely friendless, but a gap opened up and Helen Davies slipped into it, quite fluidly, allowing herself to be moved in and out according to need. It would not have happened, I'm sure—our vague, blurred friendship—if I hadn't noticed Helen in that dress that day, and wanted it more than life itself. She was simply a means to an end.

I started to find myself sitting with her and Simon sometimes, in the corner of the playground. I would take my lunch over, on the days when Myra was not there, slightly intoxicated by the way Simon stared at me with his large, wet eyes and tried to make conversation, his tongue always getting in the way. I felt so *wanted*, by them, by him and Helen, as if all the wanting I had inside me was eased by being on the receiving end of it for once. I could pretend that I was somebody that I wasn't when I was with them.

Up close, Helen and Simon had a smell about them, like wet clothes that had been left in the washing machine too long, or vase water that had gone bad. A slightly rotten, dirty-water smell that emanated from their bodies, but only when they moved in certain ways. They had identical lunches—such small square sandwiches, a piece of fruit, a biscuit wrapped in greaseproof paper—and matching black puffy schoolbags. Helen took tentative, dainty bites of the food, as if she was trying to avoid some terrible sharp thing hidden in there.

She spoke to me casually and calmly when I was with them, a touch of reproachfulness in her voice, her hands often pressed against her knees.

'Do you like Mrs Day?' she asked me one lunchtime, after we'd put our lunch boxes back in our bags. Mrs Day was our teacher, and was kind enough, but bland, not young or old, pretty or ugly; certainly not a topic of conversation.

'I guess so.'

'I like her,' said Helen, 'and Simon likes her too. He had her last year.'

Simon—always introspective unless riled—was standing beside us, twitching his fingers back and forth, sucking slightly at his bottom lip.

'Simon likes reading when he's at home,' Helen said, 'and Mrs Day lent him books out of her shelf, to bring back with him.'

She spoke slowly, as if reciting a script.

'What's your best subject?' I asked her.

Helen did not look so sure, but she answered straight away. 'I like reading too,' she said.

It must have been nearing the end of the year—in the final school term, at least—that Helen and I started playing cats and kittens, not every day, of course, but on the days when Myra was away sick and I had no one to sit with for morning tea or lunch. She asked me quite abruptly one day, her mouth still full of sandwich, Simon beside her, eating his too.

'Would you like to play cats after this?' she said, not really looking at me when she spoke, but almost directing the question at Simon. I could see the bread inside her mouth, a fleshy white pulp.

'Okay,' I said, as if I didn't care either way, though secretly I was pleased.

We went right out to the edge of the field to play it, Simon lolloping along beside us, although we hadn't invited him to be a part of the game too. Helen was wearing ordinary clothes that day, not her grey and pink striped dress, and she started getting herself ready, like a surgeon preparing for an operation. She took off her worn grey shoes and her socks, and laid them side by side, and undid the buckle of her watch—adding it to the pile—and pulled up the sleeves of her cardigan, high, so they were bunched right up above her elbows. She got herself down on all fours then, and started to meow.

Simon and I watched this whole process with a sort of dumb curiosity. I felt a faint disgust, and delight too; a desire not to look and to look at the same time. I don't know what it was that made me feel this way—perhaps just her eagerness, the methodical joy—but I knew that feeling was going to be significant, somehow, in my life.

Helen meowed and pawed at my feet with her hands, and because I actually did want to play cats and kittens with her, and because I was glad that she had chosen to be the cat, me the kitten, I leaned down and took off my shoes, and got down on all fours and started to meow and purr too. Simon just stood there, watching us, his big red hands hanging by his sides.

Once I was spending time with Helen Davies, I began to notice how Mrs Day clearly watched out for her, though in a quiet, almost secretive way. She never asked impromptu questions of her, about mathematics or spelling, like she did with the rest of us, and because Helen never put her hand up, she never had to answer questions at all. I knew about Simon and Mrs Day and the books, and sometimes I wanted to shout out that I knew during quiet reading time after lunch. There was something in Mrs Day's small grey eyes and oval fringed face that made me suspicious, as if she knew more about all of us than she would ever let on.

'And Helen can go with me!' she would say shrilly when the class had divided into even-numbered teams and Helen was the odd one out. She would get her to sit beside her then, up at her desk, and would talk to her quietly, opening and shutting the drawers, placing small things I could never get a glimpse of in Helen's out-turned hand.

*

As the term was winding up, sometime before the Christmas holidays, Helen wore her dress to school again. Perhaps that was only the second time she had worn it—the first being the day I remember noticing her—and when she walked into the classroom that morning her head seemed to be sitting very straight on her neck, quite tall. Myra was still unwell, sometimes just coming in for the mornings, so Helen and Simon and I had been spending most lunchtimes out on the field, isolated, it seemed, from the rest of the world. I felt seized by a strange joy when Helen appeared in her dress, as if I was in the company of a beautiful person, though in class I never spoke to her at all.

It was just as I had remembered—the dress—a light pink and grey stripe, a low rounded scoop neck, gathered in round the waist with a tie of the same material, little tasseled bits on its end. It was like a dress in a magazine—though it had a slightly dull, worn quality—grown up somehow, ladylike. The neckline showed off the tan of Helen's chest, which looked polished, that day, like wood.

I watched her all morning, almost infatuated. Even the ball of her hair seemed lovely, sitting above that outfit. By lunchtime, I could hardly contain the words.

'I like your dress,' I said to Helen, who was sitting with Simon in the quadrangle, waiting for me, I guess.

She smiled a small smile, and patted the material on her leg.

'Where did you get it?' I said, trying to be subtle. 'I'd like a dress like that.'

Helen took a bite of her sandwich and chewed it, and swallowed.

'We made it,' she said. 'On the machine.'

She said the words matter-of-factly, as if the topic didn't interest her at all, and when I tried to question her further, she just tucked her lunch box back into her bag, looked at me and meowed. She wanted to play cats and kittens again, and even though I was growing tired of it I agreed, not really having anywhere else to go.

*

On the last day before the Christmas holidays, the school had a special assembly in the School Hall. Myra came for the whole day, though her mother sat on the side with the teachers, and I found myself surrounded by Myra-nearly-died-in-the-hospital fans. I was like Myra's shadow, that day, and I basked in her reflected glory.

All the teachers got up one by one and handed out certificates, the names written on them in curly black loops. Myra got a Bravery Award for spending so much time in hospital—something I didn't think really deserved a *school* award—and she got up and stood in front of the whole assembly, holding the certificate in front of her chest, her white bony legs bowing outwards round the knees.

After Mrs Day had read out all the names—Most Improved Speller, Best Sportsperson—she leaned behind herself and picked up a certificate made of thick gold card.

'And finally,' she said, her voice high, quite bell-like, 'we have an award for Beautiful Behaviour, which goes to—' she paused, for dramatic effect— 'Helen Davies!'

There was a soft pattering of hands through the hall. Helen stood up and seemed to float towards Mrs Day, her feet hardly making a sound on the wooden floor.

'Congratulations, Helen!' Mrs Day said as she handed her the certificate.

Helen didn't turn towards the crowd of students sitting on the ground like everyone else had. She reached out her hand, gingerly, and without a moment's pause turned and walked back to her place, shuffling her way through the cross-legged bodies. She was sitting in between the twins, Adrian and John, who both had teeth that burst out through their lips as if they were trying to get away from the gums, and she just sat there, absolutely still, the certificate placed squarely in her lap.

*

The bell went at three o'clock that day, as always, and Myra's mother shuffled her away. It was the beginning of the summer holidays, and there seemed to be a vibration echoing around the school: excitement, and something else too, a sort of melancholy.

My mother couldn't pick me up that day, I was going to have to catch the bus, and as I walked out the school gates I spotted Helen and Simon, standing side by side by the concrete wall, waiting for something. They looked towards me, and I realised with a surge of queasiness that they were waiting for me.

'Kate!' Helen called out.

I turned slowly and deliberately towards them and walked over to where they were standing.

'Hi,' I said.

Helen was holding her certificate in one hand and in the other she had a small paper bag with little paper handles that her fingers were looped through. With her bag on her back, and both her hands occupied, she seemed even more dwarfed than usual beside enormous Simon, who had both his arms free.

'My mother says, would you like to come and play in the holidays?' she said, hardly managing to keep the words in order, her voice was so fast and breathy.

I shifted on my feet and fiddled with the edge of my sweatshirt, trying not to look at Helen's face, which was so open and filled with hope.

'I don't know if I'll be able to,' I said, though I think I muttered it really.

'My mother says she could call your mother if you're not sure,' Helen said, lifting her voice at the end of the sentence, as if it was a question, not a statement.

I felt like her need might devour me, so palpable was its quality. The sound of voices all around me seemed far away, wavering slightly, warped. The day seemed suddenly darker, though it was probably just a cloud slipping over the sun.

I didn't want to go to Helen and Simon Davies' house, which would smell, I imagined, like them, but stronger, and their mother would be there, who was so fat, someone once said, she couldn't even fit in a car. They had misunderstood. They did not understand the arrangement we'd had.

'I don't think I'll be able to,' I said.

Helen didn't seem to hear me, or if she did she didn't let on. She lifted her arm, held the paper bag out towards me.

'We found some extra in the sewing basket,' she said. 'Have a happy holiday.'

I took the bag and only glanced inside; I already knew what would be there.

'They're only off-cuts, my mother said, not enough for a dress, but I thought you'd like them anyway,' said Helen. She was still speaking so fast, as though getting all the words out was a strain.

'Thanks,' I said. 'Thanks very much. Have a happy holiday too.'

I turned instantly away from them then—Helen and Simon—and started to walk rapidly towards the bus stop, the paper bag banging against my leg. I allowed myself only one glance back before I turned the corner, and the sky seemed to go even darker when I did: a coiling darkness, like smoke. Helen and Simon were still standing by the school gate, side by side, their faces turned towards me. They were watching me go—the retreating lurch of my back—and when I glanced around they were smiling, smiling, as if I could never do them any harm at all.

In the Wind

It is all of them in the car—all of them, that is, except for Ernie (as he liked to be called), who died last month and has come along therefore in a dead way, a few handfuls of lumpy ash snap-locked inside a cobalt-blue jar. His ring is in there too, apparently, though Faith hasn't had the heart to look closely. It is molten and curled, says Nana Jo, which is odd—that it's in there—since he lost it the night he died.

'At least he doesn't need a whole seat to himself any more!' someone said as he was being placed—carefully, upright—in the boot. Faith didn't see who it was, who said it, but it was certainly either her mother or Nana Jo. Perhaps her mother, who never succeeded at being light-hearted when light-hearted was the last thing she felt.

Faith's mother sits up front wearing her back-support contraption, its many straps locked across her chest. She looks like a displaced tramper, Faith thinks, with the seat an oddly shaped pack. She is pressed so hard against it that it looks a part of her, though in reality she couldn't really tramp, considering her weight. It is a six-seater, this car, rented from the car place on Davis Street. Nana Jo is driving—which doesn't seem right at all—with Faith's mother beside her, and Faith and her brother Phil behind, his face pressed close to the pictures in a surf magazine called *Making Wavez*. Their step-sister Trudie is behind them, and her fiancé John. They talk to each other in hushed voices every now and then, and laugh softly, in a way that makes Faith feel nervous. She's glad they're behind her, rather than the other way round—that would be nauseating.

So there it is. The six of them. It is true—there wouldn't have been much room for Ernie anyway.

Outside, beyond the fences and sporadically grassed bank, the salt lakes come into view. They are a tired-looking pink, square after square of them, crystals forming on their edges. They are divided by slabs of concrete, and there is a soft mist—a soft mist that almost looks like but couldn't possibly be steam—hovering above the ones in the middle. The mist is not surprising; it is only just past dawn.

It is the beginning of July and they are on their way to the snow. Faith has taken a week's leave from her job on the outskirts of the city, where she works for a small

PR firm, and where, four months ago, she unwisely began sleeping with her (twice married) boss. He has let her take a holiday even though this is their busiest time of year. It is a simple sort of equation. She lets him slide his tanned, dark-haired hand up her skirt between business hours, and he, in turn, lets her take her leave when she wants it. A cosy wee arrangement—when you balance things up.

The car glides effortlessly over a rise in the road, where it curves a little, and they find themselves even closer, almost level with the salty ponds.

'Look,' says Faith's mother without any sign of excitement, her finger stabbing softly at the glass of the passenger window. 'Look.'

She is pointing at the salt lakes, which Faith and Nana Jo—hopefully, considering it is she who is in charge of the wheel—have already seen. Phil lifts his head away from his magazine, but drops it instantly again, not bothering even to attempt to look interested in what's outside.

'Look,' says Faith's mother again, but as she says it the car turns a corner and the salt lakes are lost from view.

*

Ernie always said he'd like to die in late spring, along with the daffodils, but he died mid-winter, which proves you don't always get what you want. In any other family he would have been called Granddad but his own Grandfather's name was Ernie and for some reason he decided that's what Faith and Phil should call him. It is ironic now, of course, Ernie being in an urn. Perhaps that had been his intention all along.

Nobody had really expected him to die when he did, though it seems now they had refused to read the signs. He *had* been in hospital for seven weeks, driving them all mad, showing no sign of going anywhere.

'I'll just wait here,' he would say to Faith as she was leaving after every visit. 'I'll just be staying here then.'

It made her laugh at the time, the absurdity of it, a man so suddenly shrunken, tubed up, feet as big as baseballs, behaving as if he actually had a say in the matter.

'Well, I'll just stay put,' he would say, without even a touch of sarcasm, his hand raised in a salute.

Of course, all he wanted was to be taken home.

*

Things with Faith and her boss have plateaued. If Faith were being honest with herself, she would even go as far as to say that things aren't going well, but she wonders if they ever do—go *well*, that is—when it comes to adultery. She has started to feel resentful. Is that really surprising? Richard—or Retch-ard, as Faith calls him, just to herself, on the bad days—has developed a way of looking at her as if he is tired and it is she who is making him so. His eyes have a slightly red-rimmed look to them, which she never noticed in the early days but has probably always been there. The redness matches the red of his gums, which he bares when he smiles, though he doesn't necessarily mean to. It is just that his teeth are somewhat stubby. Somewhat stubby, but alarmingly white. He isn't tall, or particularly handsome, and this makes Faith sometimes wonder what on earth she is doing with him. Three days ago, as he was grating his cheek against the skin of her neck, she noticed his hair thinning on the top of his head. The fact that she noticed it, and also that the top of his head was something she could see, seemed like bad signs to her. Perhaps she is only with him because he refers to her as a firecracker, which is something she has always thought she would like to be but isn't really at all.

Faith rests her head against the window. The road is surrounded by paddocks now, hilly ones that have a smattering of sheep strewn across them. Far off, pressed flat it seems against the clear skies, are the mountains, white and jagged, looking like a stage set, or at least an illusion of some kind. She feels too hot in the car. The heater is probably on full. She pulls at the neck of her jersey. She feels as if she might faint.

'Does anyone want to stop at some tearooms?' says Nana Jo, her voice characteristically jolly. She has two saunas a week and is clearly in her element temperature-wise.

'Are there tearooms close by?' says Faith's mother.

'Well, I don't know, to be honest,' says Nana Jo. 'But I thought it was worth just *throwing* the idea out there, as a possibility.'

Faith looks at her watch. It isn't even 8 a.m.

'Does anyone feel like some valium?' Phil says into the pages of his surf magazine. 'Cocaine, perhaps? Anyone? No?'

He says it quietly, but loud enough so that Faith can hear. His hair is still in a state of shock, probably from prising himself from bed so early. One side of it is as flat as a pancake, but at the back and top it sticks out jauntily, almost with flair. He looks like a parrot.

'Anyone?' he says again, his top lip leering a little at his own joke. His face is completely smooth, Faith notices, even though he turns twenty-four next month. His girlfriend has recently left him for his best friend, or some such thing. It has given his manner an edge that was never there before.

'Ah, well. All the more for me then,' he says. And all of a sudden—like a crashing sound far off, a sudden disintegration—Faith finds herself bewildered, and can't tell if he's joking, or not.

*

As children, Faith and Phil had dreamed of a skiing holiday. It was something that seemed exotic to them, just out of reach, a snowy-topped, quivering mirage. That was the ticket to success, somehow—just going for one skiing trip with your family.

Ernie may have known that, but he also may not have. Faith was never sure what he remembered and what he simply improvised. He had the serene authority and mannered charm of someone accustomed to the stage, a sense of occasion and drama in an otherwise ordinary world. When they were small he had pulled coin after coin from deep within his ear canal. It had appalled Faith at the time, this abundance of metal in people's heads. She had imagined when she moved hers too that there was a jingling deep inside—all that metal, and Ernie the only one in her life able to extract it.

Of course, he was also the only one who, until recently, had not successfully extracted himself. There had been

Faith's father who, as her mother always said, had taken off and left the three of them when Phil was only three—the matching numbers somehow detracting from the awfulness of it, moving it into a realm that was more bearable, approaching humour. Ted, of course, had had all the good intentions required, having nursed his dying wife through MS while bringing up their only daughter all alone—or so the story went—but his good intentions seemed unable to be contained within the nest. He was overflowing with good intentions wherever they were required. All that *trauma*, Faith's mother used to say good-naturedly. She said it with such emphasis that, after a while, it began to seem like a sound an animal might make: a low, drawn-out ache.

It wasn't until after Ted officially left, or after he was officially—finally—kicked out, that Faith's mother began to balloon. It was a slow, steady sort of process, as if someone, puff by puff, were blowing her up with air. She developed rolls on her neck that grew shiny with sweat on warm days. The skin round her ankles seemed to be falling over itself to get to the floor.

Faith and Phil watched the whole process with an adolescent helplessness that grew into adult helplessness over time. Ernie and Nana Jo, advocates of fruit, vegetables and yoga in the morning, must have felt a certain helplessness too.

'Your mother's body is just all brimming over with sadness,' Nana Jo said to Faith one day, a conspiratorial hush in her voice.

Faith had never felt sure if it was the brimming over, or the sadness, that was cause for such a tone. Both things seemed to be wallowing around in a shameful realm, equally fascinating and awful, like the holocaust, or a nuclear bomb.

'Be grateful for your suffering,' Faith once read on the back cover of a self-help book. 'It is the greatest gift you will ever receive.' It was true, of course. She bought it for her mother and gave her the gift of the book—advocating the gift of suffering—for her birthday. 'Gifts come in many guises!' she wrote in the card. She was trying to be light-hearted.

*

In a town with nothing in it but a store, a butcher and a cluster of tired-looking houses, Nana Jo pulls up beside a concrete block of public toilets. Nothing, it seems, is open except for the toilets, and outside of them stand a man and woman (boy and girl, really) with clipboards. One by one they all—Faith and Phil, Trudie and John, Nana Jo and Faith's mother—launch their deadened bodies out of the car and walk jaggedly across the car park like a flock of strange, misshapen birds, bent forward a little, lifting their legs and putting them down again in halting, jerky movements.

The air is cold—wet-feeling—even though the sky is perfectly blue.

Inside the toilets the cubicle doors don't lock, and there is no soap to speak of, though there are two dispensers and a coating of slime on the soap dish on the basin which certainly suggests some did exist, once. Nana Jo has brought her hairbrush in with her, but there's no mirror either. She doesn't seem put off, and instead doubles her body forward and begins to whack her head with the brush, with vigorous movements reminiscent of some sort of medieval torture. Her short, wiry crop of hair, under the wild attentions of the brush, appears to be trying to get as far away from her scalp as possible.

'Better than washing it,' Nana Jo says by means of explanation when she's finished.

When they emerge back into the morning light, the clipboarded pair slide towards them. They are doing a survey for the local council, they say, compiling satisfaction ratings of the amenities. Would they be willing to take part? Their faces seem wide and eager with hope—hers caked with a ghostly foundation that has been applied only halfway down her neck, his blooming with rosy clusters of acne. They both have deep-set eyes. Perhaps they are related.

'Will it take long?' says Nana Jo. 'We're on our way to somewhere.' She says it with such authority and self-importance that it seems she is entirely unaware of the obviousness of the statement: that a town like this would almost never be the *actual* destination. She smiles brightly at them after she's said it, encouragingly even.

They queue up, all six of them, and one by one answer the questions. When Faith's turn comes, though, she forgets to list anything of actual importance in the 'Suggestions for Improvement' section, and just mentions the lack of mirror, somehow forgetting, for that moment, the lack of soap and missing lock.

As they crawl back into the car, she asks Phil for his rating out of ten. She mimes holding a microphone out to him when she does it, which is the sort of thing that would have delighted him when he was small.

'One,' he says, with no sign of humour.

'One! So low!' says Faith, adjusting the paraphernalia around her—discarded clothes, pillows, an array of shoes—and buckling her belt.

Phil has already found his magazine, and has opened it on a poster page of an enormous claw-like wave, a dot of a man crouched beneath the froth of white.

'There was no toilet paper,' says Phil. And still no smile.

'Marlene always came first,' says Faith's mother to Nana Jo, 'but Helen was the beauty.'

The two of them have been foraging through the past— old neighbourhoods, street names—and are now onto the Martyns, who were raising their two granddaughters: their neighbours from around forty years ago. Faith has gathered this from tuning in occasionally through the cloud of her own dream-like thoughts. Everyone else in the car is in a doze too.

'With a name like that,' says Faith's mother, 'and she did look like a goddess.'

'Dead eyes, though. Not much happening between those pretty ears of hers,' Nana Jo says.

The radio, gurgling away in the background, suddenly turns to static, and instead of turning it down one of them turns the dial in the wrong direction, so that the static turns to a violent screech, just for a moment, before it is hurriedly switched off.

'Thick as a brick,' agrees Faith's mother, her voice now sounding clear and strong, only the hum of the car in the background. Nana Jo and Faith's mother make identical clacking sounds of agreement with their tongues.

'And Mr Martyn, always saying, "Will you look at that," no matter what you said to him. Remember that? You'd tell him you were on the way to town and he'd say, "Will you look at that."' When she says this, Nan Jo lowers her voice and gives it a sort of a lilt, sounding not like herself at all but presumably like Mr Martyn. 'It was as if that was his way of encouraging you, in a conversation. Funny man,' she says. 'Terribly kind.'

'Marlene used to say, "My Dad's a bad egg." All the time.'

'Not about Mr. Martyn?' Nana Jo lowers her voice even more at this, though it's clear she's just playing around.

'The father,' says Faith's mother, 'whoever he was. She'd always say it: "My Dad's a bad egg." Must've been something she overheard. Mind you, they'd know about eggs, considering all those hens.'

At this the two of them chuckle—a love of bad jokes, clearly, runs in the family—and Faith can hear her mother shifting around in her seat, re-adjusting her back-support straps.

'Marlene told me that Helen got pregnant from playing on the jungle gym too much.'

'I'll bet,' says Nana Jo.

'I believed her for a while. I was only—how old would I have been? Twelve?'

'Bless,' says Nana Jo, and the two of them fall into a sudden silence.

The silence draws Faith out of her dozing, and her eyes waver open for a moment. Outside, grassy plains stretch out on either side of the road, wide and flat, but flickering in the breeze. The grasses are a milky copper—sun bleached and parched-looking, but still bristling, undeniably alive. The car is in the base of a valley, and it feels to Faith as if they have sunk to the bottom of a bowl, hurtling along towards a certain end, surrounded by mountainous walls.

'Will you look at that,' says Nana Jo, but she says it in her own voice, not Mr Martyn's, and therefore must be referring to the mountains. It seems she has already forgotten about the Martyns and their granddaughters. The conversation has returned to the road.

*

Richard likes to send Faith emails at work that say things like, 'I'd like to tha(fuck)nk you for getting the Ellroy job finished in time.' That sort of thing. He sits behind a glass wall in their office, and after he's sent an email he watches her, waiting for the moment when she opens it. She is training herself not to react, but she must give it away somehow, because he waits for the moment so blatantly before going back to his work. He has hands which are square, roped with veins, and brown from the weekends that he spends in the garden with his wife. She, by contrast, is pearly white, oddly luminous, like frosted glass. Her name is Annie—which is, Faith thinks, the perfect name for the wife of a man one has an affair with—but he refers to her simply as A. She always wears rubber-soled ballet flats that are imported from somewhere in Spain. Not cheap, that's for sure, and always muted, tasteful blues and apricots—though once Faith saw her in a pair that were a washed-out gold. It is not that she is even particularly pretty—she has features that are small and pale also, and a slight stoop, exaggerated on the left side—but she has an effortless manner that exhausts Faith. That, and the fact that Richard has told Faith the two of them have sex in the garden (most probably amongst their well-kept hydrangea bushes) on Sundays, after they've done the mulching. He is a believer in honesty, he says, though clearly only with Faith. Jealousy is an unnecessary emotion, Richard says, which is obviously why he doesn't tell his wife about her— so that she won't be troubled with pointless thoughts.

A. is the love of his life, he says—aloof, adorable. But Faith—well, Faith is a firecracker.

Such perfect alliteration.

*

The car passes a road sign with large white lettering. They are 72 km from their destination, or so it says—their destination being the mountain, and a lodge (Nana Jo refers to it as a chalet) that they booked last week.

Inside the car it is now eerily quiet. They are filled to the brim with extraneous materials which, when they set off, appeared to be important items. Now it seems they are all at sea, utterly swamped by things that resemble rubbish more closely than they resemble anything else. Faith has misplaced one of her shoes, both of her socks and her sunglasses case. Every now and then she tries to locate them: a process that makes her look—or, rather, feel—like a long-beaked bird searching in the undergrowth for grubs. Everyone in the car reminds Faith of an animal today. She wonders if she's developing a disorder. Last week, in fact, she sat on the bus opposite a family of Swedish tourists who, alarmingly, turned into a family of guinea pigs right in front of her eyes. The little one was the first to set it off—she had such perfectly protruding teeth, and white down that matched her hair, curling its way down the edges of her hamster cheeks. Once Faith started looking— whilst, of course, trying to maintain the illusion of not looking—she realised they were all toothy, though not in an unattractive way. Cute, really. And eating nuts out of a paper bag, which only made matters worse. Guinea pigs. Or happy squirrels. Marvellously tanned.

Richard (oh, tanned one) says his favourite thing about Faith's body is her tan lines, left over from summer afternoons at the beach. Even without any clothes on, she has a little pair of white briefs etched into her skin, and two white triangles on her (not very big) breasts. They are so faint now, Faith can hardly believe they are such a stand-out for him, but it is the Playboy model look from the early 1970s, or so he says. Those girls made tan lines fashionable, coquettish, unbearably sexy. He has a collection of the vintage magazines at home which his first wife bought him, as a joke. So sexy, Richard says—and Faith never feels sure if he's referring to his first wife, the giving of the gift, or the magazines themselves. He likes the word sexy, and defines the world, somehow, by what is and isn't. He uses it in a way that unsettles Faith, as if it is some kind of liquid, perhaps a liqueur, breathily leaking out of his mouth.

Faith has tried saying it back to him—your hands are. so. sexy—but when she says the word in his presence she feels like some kind of badly animated cartoon character, perhaps with oversized shoes that trip her up whenever she tries to move. A lurch forward, followed by a stumble, inside.

*

Months before his death—did he know even then that the process was already underway?—Ernie began to compile a list of postmortem dos and don'ts. He would bring it up— his death, and the aftermath—in the most inappropriate of settings, often causing conversation to come to a standstill around him. He started up about it at a distant relative's wedding, just before dessert, and at one of Phil's birthday dinners (though perhaps that was more understandable, the link between birthdays and death at least being clear).

'Don't go packing me in under the earth,' he'd say gravely (ironic, that) when everyone else was talking house prices, or, 'Just throw me straight into the flames,' when someone mentioned the heat. He had become smaller with age, his voice, too, quite small, and as a result everyone paid less attention to him, as if he was already shrinking away into nothing, right there in his seat.

Once he was in the hospital, though, death didn't seem to interest him so much. Perhaps it was too close by then, a large but indistinct shape moving towards him. He would change the subject whenever the word arose, and this made everyone believe that it wasn't coming to get him after all. Faith discovered in herself a love for him that she'd never felt for anything else before—not even babies or injured pets. She felt it as an all-enveloping heat, a sort of a roar, filling up her entire body. She wanted to fold him up like a napkin and smuggle him out of there under her jacket. She would be flying, inside, when she walked down the corridor towards his room.

Ernie always seemed to be waiting for her, his ally, or that's how it felt. In the early days he was full of instructions the very moment she appeared by his bed: he wanted Faith to smuggle socks onto his feet, even though he wasn't allowed them in case he slipped, or he demanded to be put back in bed straight after a nurse had got him into a chair to practise sitting. His feet seemed to grow larger by the day, round and hard, the toes sticking out of them like claws. They were as cold as stone. Getting socks onto them, especially when hurrying, was almost impossible.

After a few weeks, though, he became more resigned to routine. Words seemed to matter less. Faith understood, now, what needed to be done. He knew the sound of her footsteps coming down the corridor. As soon as she caught sight of him he'd be slipping his dentures out of his mouth, holding them out to her, wanting them to be cleaned.

*

Their accommodation is not a lodge or chalet, as Nana Jo may have liked them to think, but an overpriced backpackers' swarming with Germans. The owners look tired—they work seven-day weeks, they tell Faith and her mother, and have done so, without a holiday, for ten years. Perhaps this explains—or is an attempt to excuse—why they charge like a four-star hotel, even though there are no stars (or hotels, for that matter) in sight. Both of them might have been attractive once, Faith thinks—Ken and Barbie wearing polar fleece—but everything about them misses the mark now. Her blonde hair is teased up and is set so firmly it doesn't even bounce as she walks; his has been dyed dark brown but has a plum-coloured sheen in the light. They refer to each other, humourlessly, as 'the husband' and 'the wife'.

'Childless,' Faith's mother whispers to her as they exit through the sliding door.

She turns back to smile at them after she's said it.

In the unit, Nana Jo is busy cleaning, having already piled the luggage out of the car and placed the bags, tidily, in the entrance to each room. She is using a sock—*just* an *old* sock of mine, she says—to dust the window sills, but there is no judgement or disapproval in her movement. She darts around the room, cheerily gathering the dust, and then flapping the sock outside on the porch to get rid of the excess. She is like a happy sparrow taking a dust bath, although, of course, the intention here is quite the opposite. She pats Faith supportively on the forearm as she passes her. 'What point is life if you don't make the best of it?' she once said to Faith. Faith's mother had tried to adopt this attitude, but it didn't sit so comfortably on her. There was a resentful quality to her brightness, a slight aggressiveness. It was impossible to match yourself against a happy disposition such as Nana Jo's.

—

Ernie's ashes are placed in the corner of the room. No one wants to have to look at them *all* the time, says Nana Jo. Trudie and John don't seem to want to look at them at all, subtly turning away—but towards each other—whenever they are near them. They met on a cruise ship, where they were both working for six months to pay off their student loans. John proposed to her within weeks, using the ring off a Coca-Cola can. This detail is intended to demonstrate the depth of their passion for each other, but in some company the anecdote falls flat.

'Well then,' Nana Jo had said to Trudie when she first heard. 'Are you engaged to a man or a can?'

No one except Faith had laughed.

John is in his mid-twenties, but looks sixteen, with his hair spiked up with gel and his whole being radiating the odour of spray-on supermarket cologne. He plays football, and is knotted with sinewy muscle on his top half, but his fair-haired legs have an odd shapelessness to them, a pre-pubescent look, as if he is not yet a man. He wears shorts—or cargo print three-quarters—and trainers all year round. When he laughs his shoulders jolt up and down, seemingly of their own accord. It is this, more than anything else, that irritates Faith about him. This, and the fact that when Trudie is in the room he seems incapable of making conversation with anyone—even *looking* at anyone—but her. Who on earth invited him along? He hardly knew Ernie, anyway.

There is a risk, Faith sometimes thinks to herself, that one day she may be eaten up by her own unpleasant thoughts. 'You're not just a nice girl, are you,' Richard often says to her, although he seems to say it to fulfil his own purposes, since those words come out of his mouth only when she is in a compromised position—pressed up against the refrigerator in the office kitchen with her underpants awkwardly round her knees, or folded over the photocopier like origami, Richard holding a fistful of her hair. He's beating to the sound of his own drum when he says things like that, she's sure of it. It certainly seems to get things over and done with soon enough, which, quite frankly (given the time constraints of such office exchanges), is often, quite simply, a relief.

*

In the last week of his life, Ernie decided that Nana Jo was having an affair with one of his nurses. He announced this to Faith quite matter-of-factly one afternoon, his eyebrows raised earnestly.

'She's hanging around with him, you know,' he said, opening his mouth immediately afterwards to accommodate a spoon with a mound of wobbling red jelly on it that Faith was attempting to steer towards him. He was off his food generally and the doctors were worried. He seemed no longer interested in nutrition at all, preferring the ice cream and custard, once trying to pop a little bit of it on the end of a forkful of Shepherd's pie. He had taken to hiding bits of food—the crusts on his morning toast, a floret of broccoli—between his blankets or in the drawers beside his bed.

Faith had waited for him to swallow and then, scooping up another spoonful, had asked him what he meant.

'That nurse,' he said, gesturing towards the door. 'And

your grandmother. The two of them are having it off.' He paused, patiently, waiting for Faith to cotton on to what he was saying—that the broad, hairy-armed Scottish nurse with one gold stud in his ear was indeed involved in some kind of sexual tryst with Nana Jo.

'That's ridiculous, Ernie,' said Faith.

'You're telling me!' He opened his mouth for the spoon again, and then swallowed. 'He's got it in for me now too, of course.' He breathed out, wearily—but with no emotion—and then hooked his teeth out, studied them for a moment and laid them, carefully, in the congealed mound on his plate which was presumably supposed to resemble beef stew.

That was the beginning of the end, of course. Each day there would be a new conspiracy, which he would relay to Faith with the same resigned manner. They were turning the heating up in his room, he said, to try to suffocate him, and were giving him more pills than usual, some of which were bitter, tasted like poison.

'I tried to call the papers,' he said, 'on the ward phone, but they stopped me. Of course.'

Faith would flurry around him, puffing his pillows, trying to talk some sense into him, but after a while it seemed pointless.

'Your mother and grandmother are part of all this,' he would say. 'You'll see. They're trying to knock me off my perch.'

It was truly exhausting. But his trust in Faith—and his mad, paranoid distrust of everyone else—only made her love him more.

'You're my wing man,' he would say to her, and Faith

would nod, too kind to point out to him that she wasn't a man at all. He seemed unable to differentiate by that point, once exclaiming loudly, '*He's* a big fella!' when a large Samoan woman with a flower in her hair came in to clean his room.

All of a sudden, though, he began to fade away from her—from all of them. One day he was giving her the soldier's salute and the next he couldn't be woken, and Faith, her mother and Nana Jo took shifts moistening his open mouth with a special little sponge on a stick.

The top of his head was burning hot—the Tibetans said that was what happened when someone was dying: that their soul was preparing to escape. Nana Jo told them this, her eyes wide with the wonder of folklore being borne out in this way. She seemed generally astonished by everything, but she also looked drawn and grey. Faith noticed that she was holding her own hands a lot, one palm cradling the knuckles of the other, her fingers supportively stroking the skin.

*

Nana Jo and Faith drive back into town to get supplies for dinner. The white cloud that had settled over the mountains lifts, and they see them in all their expansiveness, gleaming and sharp against the mottled plane of the sky. Their accommodation is perched at the base of the largest peak, but it is from a distance that the mountains look their best. The cloud is rolling back all along the horizon, like footage of a wave in reverse. Nana Jo hums as if she's singing along to a tune, but there's no music playing in the car.

'He'd be glad we came here,' she says.

She seems tired to Faith, although she would never admit it.

The morning before he died, Ernie woke up with a start, as if he'd slept through an alarm and suddenly realised he was late for something. He had been unconscious for twenty-four hours. He blinked rapidly, but his eyes still looked a milky blue.

'For goodness sake!' he said to himself when finally he seemed to take in the three faces peering over him. 'I'm still here.'

He couldn't get enough air—he announced this to them immediately afterwards.

'The oxygen isn't getting in like it should,' he said, and his face turned grave, a trickle of panic passing over him, tightening the skin above his lip into a small grimace.

Faith's mother went for the doctor.

'Take me up the mountain,' he said, 'as if you're going skiing.'

Nana Jo started telling him sternly that they weren't taking him anywhere, that he had to stay right there in his bed, before realising, mid-sentence, what he meant, and stammering to a halt.

'I want to go up like a stack of hay,' he said, 'and then be thrown up into the mountain air. Don't go washing me down a river like something going down the sink. I don't want to go under, I want to go up. In the wind. I can't seem to get enough air right now,' he said. 'Is someone going to help me?'

And he carried on like that for hours. Seeming to enjoy it, the process of confusing them all.

*

In the late afternoon, having returned from town with food and drinks, Faith leaves the family to their napping, and walks through the empty camping ground to a phone booth. It is cold, and the wind is getting up. The cloud is bearing down again on all of them.

She dials the office number and then Richard's extension, and feels oddly queasy just listening to the ringing tone. Richard doesn't answer. His secretary, Madeleine, does. This never happens. Faith, too surprised to realise she could actually just hang up, chokes a little, and then manages to speak.

'Faith?' says Madeleine, her voice unnaturally perky— as usual. 'I thought you were on leave?'

She is too dim ever to suspect anything. Faith can hear the sound of her fingers tapping away on the keyboard as she speaks.

'I am,' she says. 'I am. I just remembered something I needed to tell Richard—' she pauses— 'about the Macmillan file.'

'Well,' says Madeleine, taking a gulp of something, then swallowing. 'You're out of luck. Serves you right for even *thinking* about work while you're on holiday.'

'He doesn't normally leave this early.' Faith can feel the strain in her voice, like the whine of a badly tuned instrument.

'Yeah well—' other phones are ringing in the

background— 'he's gone with Annie to the doctor's.' Madeleine lowers her voice a little. 'Word on the street is that they're pregnant.'

For a moment Faith feels truly bewildered, imagining them joined together like Siamese twins, a lump, like a beach ball, growing out their conjoined stomach. Everything in her mind goes into technicolor—an image of Richard, naked, with one enormous testicle, a little foetus showing faintly through its skin. The words rattle around in her head, trying to locate sense, before they finally find their correct order and drop into place. Faith feels them fall.

Yes, that's what the words mean: that Annie has Richard's baby growing inside her; that it is his love—his loving of her—that is making that baby grow.

On the other side of the camping ground a Coke can is being bounced along the asphalt by the wind. The streets lights begin to flicker yellow—seeming for a moment like candle flames wavering in a breeze—and then all turn on at once.

*

They all get up at 6 a.m.—Nana Jo's idea—and by seven they have driven up to the ski base, and have caught the chairlifts further up the mountain. Overnight the wind has got up even more and it blows at them in alarming gusts, but the sky is blue, and this is all that matters to Nana Jo.

'A little bit of wind never hurt anybody,' she says. And she truly seems to believe that this is the case.

They are wearing snow boots and heavy jackets, and Faith's mother is lagging behind a bit, having removed her back-support brace for the first time in days. It was cutting into her skin when she wore it under her clothes, she said, so has recently taken to wearing it on top of them—having adjusted the straps, so that it will fit over her bulky sweatshirts—but this too is causing chaffing. Her back will just have to go unsupported.

Faith carries Ernie, holding him against her stomach, like a child carrying a ball. She thinks of Annie, with her stomach growing into a perfect round white moon. She tries to dismiss the thought, but it keeps trotting back to her, eager, like a dog.

Trudie is lagging behind with Faith's mother, and Nana Jo and Phil are way out front, searching, of course, for the ideal ash-scattering location. John is right behind Faith, she knows that, but she doesn't acknowledge his presence. She tries to keep her pace even, so that he won't think she's slowing down to let him catch her up. He is wearing shorts, even though they're up in the snow. This, she thinks, is reason enough to ignore him.

His voice comes towards her on a gust, surprisingly loud over her heavy breathing and the hat pulled down hard over her ears.

'Your arse is hot.'

For a moment she takes his words literally—imagines steam drifting out through her pants, heating him in her wake. Surely he couldn't mean anything other than that. She turns around, the urn suddenly heavy in her arms, her face registering shock. John slows down a little, but he keeps walking towards her. His cheeks have a boyish glow to them. He doesn't look guilty in the slightest. Perhaps she misheard. She turns around again, not saying anything, but speeds up, although the striding makes her walk feel all lopsided.

She can hear the crunch-crunch of his footsteps, jogging up behind her.

'And your tits.' He's puffing, so his voice sounds inappropriately loud, too enthusiastic to pull it all off. 'Your tits are cute too.'

Nana Jo and Phil are well ahead of them now. It is impossible to tell their dark figures apart. Faith's speed is making her jerky, her feet sinking, threatening to throw her off balance. She is filled with an astonishment that almost renders her dumb—though not for long. John is catching her up. She can see his face out of the corner of her eye. He looks extraordinarily pleased with himself, as if he's just discovered language—those words in particular—for the first time in his life.

'I don't think you should be saying that,' she says, sounding like someone she may have once known: a fearsome teacher, perhaps, at high school. 'Has it just slipped your mind? That you're almost married?' Her voice is quite low, but she knows he hears her. She feels his footsteps drop away.

She only wants to catch up to Nana Jo and Phil. She can see them—so far away—and tries calling, though her voice isn't strong any more but sounds strangled, all worn out. She tries to run then, but can feel after just a few steps that she's made a mistake. The awkwardness of Ernie is jogging in her arms. If she tries to slow down now she will slip, she knows it. She thinks that thought, and within seconds the ground responds. Her boot hits something hard, and just like a bad slapstick skit her movements go into slow motion—her eyes scan a line of black rocks jutting through the snow all around her; her arms lurch forward; and the urn does too, taking off like a bird, flying out of her hands. It hovers in the air, glowing sky-blue, and as she falls, Faith thinks, Maybe it'll just bounce.

It doesn't, of course. Between blinks, it floats, then falls onto a rock, and there are pieces of it lying everywhere on the snow. Ernie's ashes puff out into the air in a plume of dust. The wind blows them onto the snow, and onto Faith—her hair, her skin, up her nose, into her mouth.

Ernie is everywhere. Faith—down on all fours, and gasping—tries to scoop him up off the snow with her hands. The ash is not a smooth powder, as she'd imagined, but is gritty, tiny shards of bone in it like the bones in tinned salmon, or sardines.

'Can somebody help me?' she shouts. 'Can somebody help?'

Up ahead of her, Faith sees the indistinct shapes of Nana Jo and Phil pause, and when she shouts again, louder this time, she sees their bodies turn. She tries to scoop Ernie up with the shards of urn—the little pieces of bone easier to catch than the dust which, she realises, would be the powder of his skin, the few strands of hair that had remained on his head, his heart and lungs, beloved to them all, that had grown sallow and clogged with age. She spies the molten curl of his wedding ring—just a wisp of its metal, glowing against the white.

'Can somebody help?' she calls again, but the words turn into an awful choking cough, long strands of spit stringing out of her mouth and landing in bubbles on the ash. When she turns, she vaguely sees Trudie and her mother moving towards her more rapidly than she ever thought her mother could move. John has disappeared entirely, seemingly vacuumed up by the snow.

The dark figures of her family, snaking their way downhill and uphill towards her, remind her of ants—all of them, enormous ants—a broken procession of them coming to save her. Don't ants carry their dead in funeral processions too? Don't they, too, try to honour them? Nana Jo has started to run now (an extraordinary sight), and as she gets closer and closer—the colours of her clothes and her face and her boots sharpening into focus—Faith hears her voice, calling:

'A snowman! Faith? We can make him into a snowman!'

She hears the words in bursts, the jolting of Nana Jo's jog making the rhythm of them seem odd, like she's attempting to do rap.

'He would have liked it, Faith—being a snowman,' Nana Jo calls again.

Faith thinks of Annie then, even though Annie, surely, should be the last thing on her mind. It is a flash of Annie, more than a thought, coming to her with the cold seeping in through her jeans, the padding of footsteps all around her.

A jumble of pictures: Annie and her belly, the fullness of it, her ice-white skin. Then a snowman, with Ernie growing inside it, as if his cells could reacquaint themselves with each other in there, huddle together to form a little curled spine; as if he needed only to be held like that in order to start again.

Birds

I was ten when I realised my father was just an ordinary man and when I realised what that meant, for the both of us.

This was before he sold the land, and moved north to take up a job in construction, and before I went to board with the Campbells down the road.

My father and I lived on a ten-acre block 30 ks out of town. There was a long gravel driveway leading up to our house, with dark macrocarpas on one side. I liked to think of myself, at the grand age of ten, as being reasonably grown up, but I was still afraid of those trees, looming high over my head like great black hands, magpies falling down suddenly out of their branches, slicing through the air just an inch above my head. They only did this when I was hurrying down the drive, alone. I don't know if magpies can smell fear, but I swear they could tell.

I went to the small country school down the bottom of the valley; the same school my father taught at. There were slim pickings, for sure—only two teachers—but there was no doubting he was the favourite. He wore knee-high socks and shorts all year round, walking in a straight line up and down in front of the class, turning on his heel, clapping his hands. He was vaguely hopeless, which seemed exhilarating to all of us then. I held small-time celebrity status, being his son.

We had two relationships, my father and I. I called him Mr Todd five days a week, from nine to three, and he, in turn, said my name with no more emphasis, or emotion, than any of the twenty names of the other kids at school. At the end of the day I'd wait around for an hour or two, kicking a ball on the field or going through the books at the back of Miss Simpson's classroom. When he was ready, he'd go to the car and toot the horn, twice. That was the signal. We'd move seamlessly into home-time. The passenger door would be flung open, waiting for me. And he'd be waiting, too, sitting in the driver's seat, the engine running, his hands resting lightly on the wheel.

Even with my mother gone, we were doing all right. That's what I thought, anyway. And then Sal Chambers came along, and all of us were set off course.

I don't know where Sal had been before she arrived in our lives. I never got a chance to ask my father, and back then I wasn't much interested in her at all. At first she seemed like something just on the edge of my life, like a black spot on my eye, nothing big enough to worry about but not small either. It seemed to me that she simply trickled into the house, and then all of a sudden she had filled it right up. She was everywhere I looked.

She had been a nighttime visitor before she became a day one. One night I heard her laughter spiralling down the hallway, long after I had gone to bed. I'd never even laid eyes on her before this. I didn't know she existed. So it was her laugh that introduced her in a way. Long and high, sustained like an operatic note. At first I didn't know what it was, and felt a thud in my chest, as if I had heard a wild animal, something calling for its life. That's how it sounded: desperate.

This was in autumn. I know this because I remember the leaves on the ground the next day. I don't think I felt particularly troubled, I just remember—looking down and seeing them, fluttering along in front of my feet.

*

My mother left when I was five. I hardly remember her now, just a flash every now and then of her hands, pale and freckled, or the backs of her legs as she leaned down to dry her feet after swimming in the waterhole. I can't imagine having noticed such a thing when I was so small, but I feel certain there were slim spidery veins, bright blue, on the backs of her knees. And the light, watery and tinged with grey.

Perhaps my vision of my mother's legs is just that—of

plain, detail-less legs, just her leaning over, rubbing her foot with the towel. I know I can see that—her buttocks stretched quite flat, her taking care to dry between each toe—but that may be all it was. Perhaps I have added everything else in over the years; those veins belonging to some other woman, the light to another day.

It wasn't that devastating, her leaving. I was five and had just started school; felt safe there, with my father in the next room. He had always been the one who put me to bed at night and read me stories and gave me my bath. He was a hero, of sorts. He was keeping the show on the road. And my mother? I think she just couldn't cope, hated the endless paddocks and the top-dressing planes soaring over the house week after week. I think she was unwell. Not well enough to take me with her, that is.

My father and I had been alone for five years, coping fine. And then Sal Chambers came along, bringing her laughter in the middle of the night, filling me with a sudden dread, the sound ringing down the hallway and then stopping abruptly.

I said nothing to my father about it, about what I had heard, but I knew something had changed.

It wasn't for another week or two that Sal and I actually met. It was almost accidental, though I think my father had been planning it for that day. I had been next door, playing bull-rush with the McKay kids, and I came home earlier than I should have, after falling onto my chest and winding myself on the hard clay. To avoid the driveway and the magpies, I clambered over a series of fences, some of them barbed wire, paddock after paddock. I was snivelling a bit, my nose running, filling my mouth with the taste of salt.

Sal Chambers was sitting alone on the couch inside, a cup of tea between her hands. She looked up at me with an expression of odd weariness when I appeared in the doorway, as if in that moment the movements of her face were slowed down and exaggerated. She had mousey hair in a ponytail and wore baggy denim overalls. Her bare arms were almost as thin as mine. I must have looked alarming, the dirt from my fall having mixed with my few, humiliated tears, snot streaming down my lips. She looked at me for a second, blinking.

'Harry,' she said then, quite blandly, as if she had met me before, as if she knew me well.

She reminded me of a kid at school, though she must have been in her mid to late twenties. She had a smooth pale face and pointy nose. Her hair was dull and slightly limp. She was almost pretty. I remember thinking that. That compared to Miss Simpson and Mrs McKay and Mrs Campbell she was, almost, half pretty.

That autumn the winds came. Sometimes I felt that the arrival of the wind, and the arrival of Sal Chambers' wild laugh, were one and the same. That somehow a shell had been cracked, and all the noise was pouring forth. We were not used to wind like that, especially not at that time of year; it was not normal, as my father said. It would come out of nowhere, gale force, whipping the scattered leaves into a frenzy, carrying a watering can and piece of tarpaulin, once, all the way down our drive. My father and I started tying things down with rope.

'We should tie the bloody roof down!' he said, grinning as if it was all a great joke. Nothing could dampen his spirits.

Sal was working at Arbuckle's Nursery, just round the corner from the pub. I don't know where she was living, she only ever came to our house, and as time went on it seemed she did that more and more often. She always wore overalls, denim, khaki-green, and tight little teeshirts underneath that showed the smallness of her shoulders and the top of her narrow back. Her laugh seemed quite absurd, coming out of that head and thin-lipped mouth like a roar coming out of a mouse.

My father, who had always been absent minded in a cheery, inoffensive way, seemed to totally lose his head. He was not my teacher that year—I was in Miss Simpson's class—but when I saw him round school he had a slightly daft expression on his face, as if he was somewhere else entirely.

At home he tried to butter me up. I think he felt bad, could feel himself losing a hold on his role as a consistent, stable father. I realise now that he was actually still quite young, thirty-five at the most, and that he had a right, with or without me, to have a life too. This was beyond comprehension to me at the age of ten, and as I have said, it wasn't that at that point it seemed devastatingly huge to me. It was just strange.

During the weekdays Sal came over every evening after she had finished work. She drove a small, beat-up hatchback that looked a little like a beetle. I would hear the clunking of the engine coming down the drive long before she pulled up in front of the house. I would feel a slight sinking in my stomach every time.

Despite her laugh, her voice was soft and girlish. She would talk to my father in the kitchen and I would never be able to hear what she was saying. It was a sweet voice, I guess, the voice of someone who would never intend to do harm. Sometimes when we ate dinner round the table she would try to talk to me, ask a question, her head bobbing slightly as she spoke. Somehow her questions seemed unanswerable, although I always did my best.

'What do *you* think of this wind?' she would say, her head wobbling slightly on her neck, her light-grey eyes surveying the room, not me.

'That's you, Harry,' my father would say, grinning idiotically, pointing his fork. 'That's a question for you.' He was relieved, I think, whenever she made an attempt to talk to me. I suppose he hoped we could become great friends.

*

That year I got my first real crush on a girl. Her name was Bronwyn James and she was the Campbells' niece. She was living with them for the year because her parents had gone overseas. She was fifteen. She caught the bus with the older kids every day to the high school in town.

It was an innocent crush on my part, and utterly hopeless, of course. Bronwyn was not only five years older than me, but she had the gangly charm of a girl who looked unnervingly grown up, whose body seemed to be one step ahead of the rest of her. She had long sandy hair and so many freckles they merged with her skin, making her look almost tanned.

She took a liking to me in a maternal, abstracted sort of way.

I would see Bronwyn whenever all us kids went down to the swimming hole on Grange Road, usually on Sundays. She would be there too, often with a book, sitting on the rough clay of the bank with her knees up. She had a pale-blue swimsuit with a slight silver sheen. When she rose up out of the water, the water would fall off her in a way that it seemed to me it didn't do with any of the rest of us. It was as if, for a moment, she was liquid too, slippery as a seal.

I don't think my awe of her was entirely innocent, but my fascination with her body was more with the foreignness of it, the novelty factor of having a friend whose legs and chest curved like that. There was something exhilarating—something I was yet to really understand—about being in the company of someone who moved their limbs so slowly, with such deft control. She would roll her damp towel into a turban on the top of her head, her wet hair curled in its middle, and my chest would do a little hiccup inside.

'Come sit next to me, Harry,' she would say sometimes when I was standing, shivering in the wind, on the bank. She would share an apple with me out of her canvas bag. She felt sorry for me, I realise now, me having no mother and all.

It must have been a couple of months into my father's relationship with Sal Chambers that I first started to grasp what an adult relationship really meant. Perhaps, as country kids, we were all especially innocent and unsophisticated. We knew what sex was, I think, but didn't really understand that it wasn't purely a device for breeding. Someone at school had heard somewhere that you had to have sex twice in order to have a baby. Jimmy Rogers was one of six, and we all laughed at him: that would have meant his parents had had sex *twelve* times. I was the luckiest of all: mine had only had it twice.

I knew that Sal slept in my father's bed with him, and that there seemed to be a vibration, something almost electrical, in the way they moved around each other in the kitchen, as if there was a magnetic force that locked their limbs, hands, sides together, when they least expected it. I knew that much. It made me feel odd coming across my father brushing his hand, lightly, across Sal's bottom; the way she turned and looked at him when he did it, the expression on her narrow face almost defiant.

I came across them one night long after I should have been asleep. The wind was up again, making the whole house quake, the rose bush outside my bedroom window scratching its dry thorns across the glass. I felt agitated by the noise, and scared, though I don't really know what of.

I got up and opened my door quietly, careful not to make it creak. It was nearly midnight and I expected my father and Sal to be asleep, but the living-room door was ajar, and a triangle of light lay on the hallway carpet. I should have turned around and gone back to bed, comforted by the knowledge that my father was still in the house, but something wouldn't let me, and I walked towards the light, slowly and cautiously, drawn towards the golden hum like a bee.

My father and Sal Chambers were in the living room, by the mantelpiece. Sal's elbows were resting on it, her overalls and underpants around her ankles. Her teeshirt was pulled up awkwardly, exposing one side of her back. My father was pressed hard against her. His pants were half on, half off, and the buckle of his belt jingled, flapping rhythmically against his thigh.

He was banging his whole body against her back.

Out of Sal's mouth came a muffled crying, like an injured dog, and it seemed to me then, standing in the doorway in my cold bare feet, that Sal was in pain, and that it was my father who was causing it, it was my father who was hurting her.

*

Autumn slid into winter. The winds died down. They were replaced by frosty still days, the sky a cool blue, the grass always crisp in the morning.

Sal didn't bring any belongings with her, she never officially moved in, but she seemed always to be around, miraculously surfacing in the morning, even if I'd never seen her arrive at night. She ate muesli for breakfast, floating in so much milk it looked like soup, and she still tried, in her strange detached way, to form some kind of friendly alliance with me. The unanswerable questions continued.

'Seven letters,' she said to me one morning, sitting at the table with the crossword in her lap. 'Organic or natural. Seven letters. Any ideas?'

I had none, and had a mouthful of toast. I shook my head.

Sal glanced at my face, her cool slanted eyes expressionless, and then she smiled quietly, as if she liked what she saw, or found it amusing at least. She picked up her pencil and went back to scribbling words on the corner of the paper.

As it grew colder, I saw Bronwyn James less and less. She was above playing bull-rush or tag with us, and the swimming hole no longer provided a meeting place, the murky water's edge often being laced with ice in the mornings.

I came across her one afternoon riding her horse down the road. I was on my way home, and heard the clipping of its hooves moving along behind me, getting louder with every step. She drew up beside me and tilted her chin.

'Haven't seen you around,' she said, looking down at me from a great height, her knees and feet level with the top of my head. The horse snorted and stamped one foot.

I agreed with her; we hadn't seen each other for ages.

Bronwyn smiled, and bowed her head down towards me so she looked like she could slide right off the horse's back and land on my shoulder.

'You know, Harry,' she said, the corner of her mouth twisting into a smile, 'I kinda miss you when you're not around.'

The world seemed to go deathly quiet at that moment, as if all of the air had been sucked out of it. Bronwyn laughed, and then she kicked her heel and took off at a gallop.

I stood in the middle of the road, watching her bounce

away, my chest thumping in time with her long ropey plait. I don't know if she was teasing, or serious, but for days afterward I carried the knowledge of those words, believing that when I was old enough Bronwyn and I could get married, that we could ride off together into the sunset.

*

Things with my father and Sal Chambers didn't have a notable decline. Perhaps after a couple of months, once we were through autumn and winter, once the daffodils had started poking their heads through the grass, their relationship seemed cooler somehow, but that was a relief to me, rather than a disappointment.

Sal was still at our house most of the time, and I was still wishing she wasn't.

It must have been nearing November, on a blustery Sunday afternoon, that it finally became clear to me that my father didn't think the world of Sal after all.

She wanted to go on a day trip, she was determined, so the three of us piled into the car and drove forty minutes to the sea. It was the first time I had ever seen Sal wearing anything other than overalls. She had shorts on that day, and a light knitted cardigan. I could see her knees from the back seat, knobbly and slightly pink. For the entire drive nobody spoke, and every now and then my father scratched the back of his head irritably, as if there was something under the hair that he wanted to get rid of. Sal had her elbow resting by the window, and looked out it, her palm pressed against her cheek.

When we arrived it was clear that it hadn't been a good idea, coming to the sea, just as my father had said. From the car park, still buckled up inside the car, we could see that it was exposed and windy, the grey waves roaring, sand rolling in airborne wheels along the beach. It would get in our eyes, my father said, if we tried to walk down by the water. A muscle twitched in his jaw.

'Does Harry think it was a bad idea coming?' Sal said casually, staring straight ahead out through the windscreen. 'Harry? Do you think it was a bad idea?'

I said no with as much conviction as I could muster.

'Well, then,' she said.

My father tried to smile brightly, and put on his running shoes, and the three of us loped across the driftwood, up onto the grass leading to the cliff-tops. Sal walked with her hands on her hips, hopping across the rocks like a sparrow.

The grass was long and scratchy, bending double in the wind. It almost came up to my knees. I felt like I was wading through water. It was steep, going up, and my father puffed a little. You couldn't hear it, his heavy breathing, not above the sound of the wind, but when he turned to smile at me, to make sure I was keeping up, his chest was rising and falling faster and harder than normal, and his cheeks had a rush of pink. Sal seemed to be having no trouble at all. She whistled as if it was all great fun, and swung her arms.

I'd only ever been to the cliff-tops twice before, and they seemed slightly threatening to me, as if, no matter how far away you were from the edge, you could still fall off. Years later a man tried to kill himself up there, and failed. He mashed his brains and broke his back, and never uttered another word, not even his own name.

On that day, high up there in the whipping wind, all three of us stayed as inland as we could, without crossing the fences that led to the coastal farms and the small seaside town beyond them. We could only see the far horizon of the sea, where it looked quite calm and flat, and the sky above it.

We must have been nearing the top when my father tripped, going over on his ankle and stumbling, half falling, a little down the slope towards me. For a moment he looked comic, his face ruddy, his limbs all going in different directions, looking boneless, like soft rubber.

Sal began to laugh.

I don't think she meant to be cruel. I think it was just that he did look funny, for a moment, and she lost a hold of herself, up there above the sea, right in the middle of that wind. She screeched with laughter, her lips spread back across her gums, almost in a grimace. She staggered a little, she was laughing so much.

My father was hurt and puffing and his face went redder and redder. He examined his ankle, and puffed and grunted. Sal continued to laugh, louder and more hysterically, her feet going round in circles, the sound on an ebb and flow with the wind. I stood in one spot and stared, not sure what the right thing was to do.

'Stop it,' my father said to Sal, quietly at first, trying hard to steady his voice. 'Stop it.'

In her writhing stumbling dance, her mouth still open, the sound still coming out, Sal tried to shake her head, but she only laughed more, bending over double.

'Stop it, Sal,' my father said, louder this time, with more force. 'I'm asking you please. Stop it.'

She didn't.

He moved towards her, lurching on his bad foot, and she didn't step away, just lifted her head to look at him, her laugh so airless now it sounded like she was crying, her hand on her forehead to steady herself.

'Stop it,' my father said again.

I looked down back where we had come from, at the grass bending in the wind, and a square of sand, driftwood scattered across it, the car park with our lone car on it, a dull green the size of my thumb. When I looked back, my father's arm was mid-air, moving towards Sal's face, and then his knuckles were against her teeth, hard, were skating upwards, dragging her lip with them, right up into her nose.

She fell back onto the grass, heavily, and said, 'Oh,' as if she had dropped something that didn't really matter. 'Oh,' she said again, and then, 'Goodness.'

My father stood beside her, breathing, and I breathed suddenly fast too.

We all stayed stock still for a moment. And then the blood came. It came out her mouth and out her nose, and she said, 'Oh goodness,' again, still quite calmly, one hand cupping the blood under her chin, the other making a little roof over her nose.

My father had never hit me as a child and he had never hit any of the children at school, and I don't think he'd meant to hit Sal either, just to stop her laughing, but he was suddenly white, bone quiet, as if he'd killed her.

'It's okay,' he said. 'It's okay,' sounding as if he didn't

mean it at all. 'Harry, stay here. Stay. I'll get a rag. Stay, Harry. Sal—' he paused— 'it's okay.'

And then he was off, half running, limping, staggering down the slope, passing me, not even looking me in the face.

'It's okay,' he kept calling out as he disappeared from view, his voice coming and going, battered by the wind.

I stood facing Sal and Sal faced me, the blood snaking down her neck and over her hands and onto the sleeves of her cardigan.

'Oh, Harry,' she said.

I had no choice. I moved up the slope towards this woman whom I'd never even wanted to know, and stood beside her, facing the car park, so I could look out for my father. A flock of gulls flew over our heads then, quite low, crying out, their wings beating the air. And it occurred to me, just at that moment, that all of their voices together, rippling in the wind, sounded like Sal's laughter—that they *were* her laughter—and that they were carrying it away. Sal looked up and I looked up, and then they were gone. There was only the sound of the wind and the grass and the sea, as if it was far away.

'What did he do that for?' Sal said in her bland, quiet voice. 'What did he mean by that, Harry?'

It was the last unanswerable question she ever asked me. I didn't know why my father had done it, but I knew he hadn't meant it, not really. Sal was shaking a bit, and because I had nothing to say, I lifted my two hands and placed them side by side on the top of her head, holding her, if you like, like a ball. It was an odd thing to do, I think now, but right then it seemed be the only thing that was right, and she let me, Sal Chambers, keeping her head quite still, despite all that rushing blood.

The wind whipped at our clothes, and seemed to get in under them so that I suddenly felt cold. I could see my father moving across the sand, dodging the driftwood, up towards the car park.

'What did he do that for?' Sal said again, almost in a whisper, not asking me now, but asking the grass, it seemed, and the wind and the sky.

I pressed my hands a little tighter, and felt the slight pulse of her skull under my palms, the softness and the hardness of it, like an eggshell. I looked out for my father, whom I could no longer see. There was only the bare sand, and the driftwood and the car park with our small round car.

Sal shifted slightly under my hands, and a gust of wind blew a few dots of blood onto my leg.

'Why did he *do* that?' Sal said again, just to herself. She put her hand inside her mouth, and felt her tooth, and said, 'Oh Jesus.'

'Oh Christ,' she said. I think she may have been crying.

I stared steadily out at the car park and at our car, the grey strip of sea to my left, Sal's small narrow head beneath my hands. I waited there, seemingly on the edge of the world, for my father to come back, and make it all okay.

Acknowledgements

I would like to thank Bill Manhire, for your wonderful teaching and encouragement during the writing of the first draft of this book, and Fergus Barrowman, for your patience and kindness.

For editorial advice and insight—offered with such gentleness and care—thank you Jane Parkin.

Thank you to the class of 2006 for your continuing support and friendship: Craig Cliff, Gigi Fenster, Tom Fitzsimons, Emma Gallagher, Kate Mahony, Mary Macpherson, Lucy Orbell, Sue Orr, and Abby Stewart.

Thank you Denis and Verna Adam, Biddy Grant, and my grandmother Bobbie Taylor, for financially enabling me to complete this book.

Many thanks, also, to Victoria Birkinshaw, Gina Kiel and Harry A'Court for working on the cover, and to Mark Derby for ongoing support, Christine and Adrian Taylor for providing a country writing retreat, and all my much loved family and friends (especially the Bidwill five).

And finally, this book belongs to three people:

My mother, Erin, who is always my first and most trusted reader and critic. You have stood beside me offering insights, ideas, and constant energy and enthusiasm. Thank you for graciously allowing me to weave your real life experience into a story in 'The Beekeeper'. This book would not have been possible without you.

Loren, who made the diorama on the cover, and who has spent many hours supporting and encouraging the writing of these stories as they limped into life. I feel blessed to have such an affirming and loving sister as you.

And Dylan, my love, who has tirelessly driven me on when I've been close to giving up on the book altogether. You never fail to make me feel happy, no matter how dreary the day has been.

I am indebted to all three of you.

Thank you.